Crusader's Gold

(Alicia Myles #2)

By

David Leadbeater

Thriller, adventure, action, mystery, suspense, archaeological, military, historical

Other Books by David Leadbeater:

The Matt Drake Series
The Bones of Odin (Matt Drake #1)
The Blood King Conspiracy (Matt Drake #2)
The Gates of hell (Matt Drake 3)
The Tomb of the Gods (Matt Drake #4)
Brothers in Arms (Matt Drake #5)
The Swords of Babylon (Matt Drake #6)
Blood Vengeance (Matt Drake #7)
Last Man Standing (Matt Drake #8)
The Plagues of Pandora (Matt Drake #9)
The Lost Kingdom (Matt Drake #10)

The Alicia Myles Series
Aztec Gold (Alicia Myles #1)

The Disavowed Series:
The Razor's Edge (Disavowed #1)
In Harm's Way (Disavowed #2)
Threat Level: Red (Disavowed #3)

The Chosen Few Series
Chosen (The Chosen Trilogy #1)
Guardians (The Chosen Tribology #2)

Short Stories
Walking with Ghosts (A short story)
A Whispering of Ghosts (A short story)

Connect with the author on Twitter: @dleadbeater2011
Visit the author's website: www.davidleadbeater.com

All helpful, genuine comments are welcome. I would love to hear from you.
davidleadbeater2011@hotmail.co.uk

<u>DEDICATION</u>

For Chris.

I hope you're happy, mate. Wherever you are.

PROLOGUE

Constantinople—April 12, 1204

The young Antonio Rambaldo paused and rested his scarred hands against the rough, damp city wall. Did she still breathe? Was she panicked? Was her great heart quailing at the thought of what was soon to come? By the mood in the camp today, she should.

The weather conditions had finally favored them. Venetian ships were coming close to the walls. Crusaders were already entering the city. It was over six months since they had arrived at this place and the Byzantine Empire was about to feel the full wrath of the Christians. Rambaldo hefted his sword and looked about. Grim-faced men stood everywhere—faces dirty, pockmarked, resolute. Their leader, the half-crazy, blind and heavily-aged Doge of Venice, Enrico Dandolo, led them into this greatest battle of battles.

The wall was breached, the crusaders crawling through holes they could barely fit into. Bloody fighting continued along the walls above. Ragged bodies fell all around. The Varangians would not give up easily. Rambaldo took his turn, angling his body into the rough hole and bending almost double. The sound of battle faded, replaced by the harsh grunting of weary but determined men. Their goal was now but a stone's throw away.

Swords and helmets grated harshly against the walls. A circle of light, an exit, appeared ahead, filled by blood-covered men readying weapons. Crusaders fell out of the end of the hole, body after body, man after man, until their swelling numbers began to make a difference.

Rambaldo climbed over the still-warm, still-screaming bodies of his Venetian comrades, instantly faced by an axe-wielder, an Anglo-Saxon by the look of him. Rambaldo took the axe blow on his sword, deflected it and sliced at the snarling face. Blood flew. The crusader was able to get his first real look at the city of Constantinople, the city that stood in their way on their march to the Holy Land.

Constantinople had become a genuine museum of ancient art and history; a lavish home of opulent wealth, a Byzantine playground. The Latins were shocked at what they saw and would find, but not as shocked as they were becoming by their fellow French and similar Catholic crusaders who slew indiscriminately, pausing only to drink wine, rape and murder priests.

Rambaldo forged his way further into the city, fighting only when he was forced to, trying to follow the path shaped by his blind Doge, Dandolo, and to stick with fellow Venetians who wanted none of this terrible pillaging.

Toward the great church they strove. The Venetians were themselves semi-Byzantines and wanted to save the greatest art from the rampagers. And other crusaders would not dare challenge Dandolo, a man as shrewd as he was both brave and pious, he had become a leader in his mid-seventies, performing tremendous mental and physical acts and, since the Venetians were funding this, the Fourth Crusade, was well known to be its most influential figure.

Rambaldo reached the great Hagia Sophia some time after the first groups, caught up in battle along the way. The defenders grouped together and launched attack after attack on the invaders even as their walls were breached and began to fall, even as the Blachernae section of the city was captured and used as a base to attack its remainder, even as a great fire began to rage among thousands of homes.

The skies groaned, burning bright, stormy with smoke as the great library was destroyed; other churches and monasteries were razed as the defilers stole all they could lay their hands upon, eyes and brains blinded by the promised rewards of thousands of silver marks.

Rambaldo finally stood in the shadow of the great church. The Hagia Sophia was like nothing he had ever seen before, dwarfing even the image he had kept in his imagination, and over seven hundred years old.

Gnarled fingers tightly gripped the hilt of his sword. The disgrace of it all was—the crusaders had originally been granted safe passage through Constantinople on their way to Jerusalem, a deal changed by the death of its emperor. It was only after this that Dandolo and his generals decided to sack the city itself, in an attempt to set up a new Latin Empire.

Rambaldo approached the steps of Hagia Sophia, surrounded by his fellows, walking through small fires that burned around the concrete, some the remains of art and literature and expensive cloths, others the remains of people.

Rambaldo eyed the destruction, the blatant and often gleeful carnage, with a world-weary eye. Many times during his half-century life he had been called upon to be a soldier, each time inuring him to the excesses of the next. Each return made it harder to reconnect to his wife, his growing children. War and battle changed a man, but twenty five years of it turned him into an entirely different creature. Rambaldo had tried desperately to hold on to his humanity but, until now, had always thought he'd failed.

And yet, the actions of the other crusaders showed that it was they who were no longer human, not the Venetians.

Ahead, Dandolo halted, staring across the way toward the great, awe-inspiring Hippodrome, a large chariot racing track looked over by the four great gilt horses created by the world's greatest known sculptor, Lysippos, sometime in the fourth century BCE. Rambaldo noted that his commander appeared rapt, even overwhelmed, and quickly sent a contingent of men in that direction. Rambaldo also reminded himself that his commander was blind. Dandolo had to have known what he wanted—the stare was purely for show.

They crossed the square and made to enter the great religious center of Hagia Sophia; many of the Venetian crusaders almost overawed to be in her shadow, others struggling to stay close to their great commander, Dandolo. It was then that a wave of enemy combatants swept in from the tree line to the right. Rambaldo saw the bloody battle about to erupt and once more hardened his heart, distanced his emotions and narrowed his vision.

Hagia Sophia itself watched over it all like an indifferent deity. Indeed, it had seen it all before. Twice destroyed and rebuilt, it had once been said that 'God allowed the mob to commit this sacrilege, knowing how great the beauty of this church would be when restored.' Today however, it was a complex affair and though some crusaders were indeed ransacking and defiling the great church, others were defending its sanctity and still others were stood wondering why those who rampaged seemed to have forgotten that Constantinople was only the gateway to Jerusalem, not the task that Pope Innocent III had first set them upon. Worse, they were plundering the very living treasures of the church. The catastrophic effects would ricochet down throughout history.

Rambaldo stood his ground, taking blows, resigned by now that every battle might be his last. Yes, he wanted to survive this day, yes he wanted to see Jerusalem, and yes he even wanted to return to his homeland where his wife at least awaited him, but a man so jaded as he would not be unwelcoming to the sharp stab of quick release. Some men dropped around him, but the crusaders were a battle-hardened lot and this batch of defenders were not. Soon, Rambaldo turned his attention back once again to the church and entered only to find Dandolo on his knees. At first fearful, but then acutely aware, he stared around at the desecrations that had already been wrought by the defilers.

Silver iconostasis—icons holding the holy books of Hagia Sophia—had been overturned and smashed to pieces. Seated upon the patriarchal throne was a naked whore, singing coarse songs. Crusaders stood around in their wicked bawdiness, drinking wine from the church's holy cups. Bodies littered the floor and a priest had been draped upon a hanging tapestry, his flesh defiled. They were destroying the holy altar, herding horses and mules into the church to better carry off its holiest of treasures.

And here we stand, Rambaldo thought. *Brave Christians all. Liberating this Christian city from its Christian rulers in the name of Christianity. Religion at its most crazy.*

In future years he hoped the world might get better.

The noise inside Hagia Sophia was raucous, riotous. Dandolo appeared to wilt, possibly realizing immediately that even he could do naught to dissuade the crusaders from their damaging path. In another moment the Doge seemed to come to a decision, waving his men away from the hall and toward sparser areas.

"If we cannot save all her history," he said aloud, "along with the remainder of this great city's, then we can preserve only its finest."

Rambaldo thought of the Hippodrome and its famous horses and wondered what Dandolo had in mind for them. How had the Doge come by such secret knowledge? Of course the answer stared him immediately in the face—many years earlier, before becoming the 42nd Doge of Venice, Dandolo had been appointed ambassador to Constantinople, charged with the thankless task of settling Venice's disputes through diplomatic settlements. His many visits would have led to familiarity, acquaintance and the inevitable learning of secrets. Back then, of course, his sight had not been afflicted.

And the siege and final sacking of Constantinople was granted through his direction.

Rambaldo followed his leader deep into the great church, at one point twisting around to the exterior and re-entering through a smaller barred gate until all was in silence and a deep, fetid air permeated the small space in which they were gathered. Before them lay the entrance to a catacomb and the rumbling rush of deep water.

Were there secret passages underneath Hagia Sophia?

Dandolo, though blind, appeared to know exactly where he was going.

Rambaldo followed with thirty other knights, seeking the treasure of treasures.

ONE

Michael Crouch heard his cellphone ringing and sent his hand fumbling through his pockets to try and find it.

Caitlyn Nash held it out at arm's length, not looking at Crouch but carrying on her conversation with Zack Healey.

Crouch shook his head a little. "Thanks."

He checked the screen. The call was from Rolland Sadler, his new team's wealthy benefactor—the man who funded their treasure hunting expeditions.

"Hello, Rolland."

"Michael. I hear you're over in America helping Greg Coker out of a sticky situation. Isn't he the man who tried to have you all killed recently?"

Crouch laughed quietly. "You're certainly well informed, Rolland. I wasn't aware anyone other than Alicia knew what we were up to."

"Ah, the incomparable Miss Myles. I hear she helped save Mai Kitano recently. Has she returned yet?"

Crouch hesitated. "Not yet."

"I know of her loss during that mission. Perhaps she decided to stay for the funeral."

Crouch stared into the middle-distance. "Perhaps, but unlikely. Alicia's instinct would be to move on as fast as she possibly could. I've been waiting for a good enough excuse to contact her."

"Then I'm even happier I called. Have you finished your . . . um . . . business with Coker?"

"Greg's fine. The hired goons who were watching and intimidating his family refused to give up even after we took care of their boss over in South Africa. The problem has now been resolved."

"Excellent. Then I believe I may have a new quest for you, Michael."

Crouch immediately felt a thrill course through his veins. All his life he had been awaiting this new adventure. Though an extremely capable soldier and even more highly regarded leader Crouch's real love had always been founded in archaeological mysteries. The life of a soldier had been his job, his responsibility, but his real calling lay with the hunting down and discovery of ancient treasure, so when the chance came, as Crouch hit his fifties, he embraced it with his entire being. He set up a trusted crew, a group of fighters and investigators, and listened to what Rolland Sadler had to say. Crouch, a sentimentalist at heart, stored and remembered details of every lost treasure he'd ever investigated—now the old, half-serious potterings were starting to bear wholesome fruit.

"You have my attention, Rolland."

"I thought I might. Let me first paint a picture for you—a crusader army marching to liberate Jerusalem. Invited to take a short cut through Constantinople. Arriving there, they are told they no longer have passage . . ."

"The Fourth Crusade," Crouch said, "that led to the sacking of Constantinople and the downfall of the Byzantine Empire."

"Among many other things. The sack of Constantinople was a turning point in history. One of the first and irrefutable proofs that many who fight in the name of religion are actually full of shit."

"Even the Pope condemned it as I remember." Crouch thought back through a lifetime of studies. "Some of the world's greatest treasures destroyed or lost forever."

"Just so. Well, as you know Constantinople is now called Istanbul. You may have heard that the site where the ancient docks once stood has recently been uncovered over there. A new road was being built, I believe, which unearthed the historical site exactly where archaeologists always said it was . . ." a note of quiet satisfaction crept into Sadler's voice. "So, no more road and a great dig gets underway."

"Really?" Crouch was surprised.

"No. Of course not. The road, its money men and the government wouldn't stand for that. Our unique ancient site is due to be filled with concrete and the archaeologists have but a few weeks to find whatever they can."

Crouch nodded silently. Realizing now that this call was another turning point he took a seat at the table. His current team, Caitlyn, Healey and Rob Russo had met this morning at a local Denny's for breakfast. The blueberry pancakes were as good as ever, the hash browns a tasty side and the coffee mellow, hot and plentiful.

"So what have they found, Rolland?"

"I can't say too much at this point, Michael. What I really need is you and your team on a plane, headed for Istanbul. We don't have much time. Can you do that?"

Crouch wondered at Sadler's reticence. Was the find that valuable? And if so, why did they need a team that hunted for lost treasures? Clearly, there was an awful lot being left unsaid. "Of course. We can be on a plane in a matter of hours. I'll have to check Alicia's status first—"

Heads were swiveling toward him, none larger or harder than Russo's. The movement was as deliberate and slow as an ancient stone statue coming to life.

"They found something under those docks, Michael. Something astounding."

"How astounding?"

"It will rewrite parts of history."

"Bloody hell. Now you've piqued my interest. But how can it be lost, and can't you tell me more?"

"Just remember your history around 1200 AD. Alexandria being attacked and the Hippodrome of Constantinople. The Fourth Crusade and the Doge of Venice. The best known wonder that he stole. And get on that plane."

Crouch's head was a swirling constellation of memories and suppositions. How on earth could an ancient, newly found dock in Istanbul be connected to an attack on Alexandria—of which there had been countless throughout history—and then the old Hippodrome? Where did that fit with the crusaders? And what the hell did the Doge steal that Sadler seemed to think was so famous?

"All right, Rolland. I'll call you when we're in the air."

Crouch glanced across at his crew. "Hope you weren't planning on finishing those meals, guys. We have a new treasure to seek out."

Russo sighed at the stack of pancakes before him. Caitlyn smiled. "When you say new—do you really mean old?"

"I guess I do."

"And you mentioned contacting Alicia," Russo said warily. "Does that mean we're actually working with Her Craziness again? 'Cause I gotta say, the last few weeks have been comparatively sane."

"Are you saying she's irrational? I seem to remember thinking you worked well together in the end."

"I'm not convinced she's a leader."

Crouch was surprised but not unhappy to see such a verbose Russo. The man-mountain was usually as quiet as his description made him sound.

"I think she's about to surprise you. Surprise everyone, actually. It's been a long time coming, but that girl is about to have a revelation."

Russo hung his head. "Shit. So long as I'm not on the receiving end."

"Somebody will be. You can be sure of that."

Russo nodded at his dripping pancakes. "I know."

Crouch stared out the window into a bright, fresh dawn. "Destiny awaits, my friends. I must admit, things have been a little quiet since we rounded off the Aztec quest. Are you ready to taste the adventure again?"

Healey's young, fresh face split into a wide grin. "Always!"

Crouch headed for the door. "Then follow me."

Russo's grumble followed him out toward the parking lot. "Whoa, you forgot to pay. Oh, bollocks . . ."

TWO

Alicia Myles shifted her legs in an attempt to iron out the cramps, feeling the pinch of economy class air travel. She had never understood why the goons who designed airplanes didn't make them a few feet wider instead of barely wide enough to fit ten across. Every passenger in the world would surely pay an extra few dollars to offset the extra cost, so the airlines would soon earn their money back. Everyone's happy. Maybe it was all down to the money men, the string-pullers, the ones who always travelled first class.

Ahhhh . . .

Trying to rein in her bitter outlook, Alicia found her thoughts snapping back to more recent events, but that wouldn't do. Shit, that wouldn't do at all. Her latest exhausting escapade had involved returning to the SPEAR team for a few weeks, saving Mai Kitano's ass and searching out a lost kingdom. She had also gotten to dress up like Jennifer Lawrence at an *X-Men* premiere. *Great for an hour or two,* she thought. *But it's nothing but bollocks in the real schemes of honest life. I couldn't do that more than once. Maybe twice.*

Then she remembered how it all ended. The dark alleyway. The lifeless body of their great friend and fellow soldier, and all the warriors seated at his side, sharing their final thoughts and the profound, silent night with him before the last moment was lost to eternity.

Water filled her eyes.

Perhaps it was the airplane's air conditioning, the recirc system not functioning properly. Alicia fought it off by focusing on where she was going and what might happen next. The Kindle HD on her lap was set to 'airplane' mode and she'd just received a message through the plane's Wi-Fi from her boss, Michael Crouch.

'Call as soon as you can. New mission in Istanbul. Meet you there?'

Alicia felt a small rush of happiness for the first time in days. A new mission was exactly what she needed right now and yes, the bruises, cuts and sprains from her last battle might not have healed yet, but the mental wounds would never heal. Best to lay them behind her. Best to move on. Flesh would take care of itself. The mind—that was a far larger problem, one she'd been struggling with for the best part of her life.

She thought about where she was headed. And where was that? Oh yeah . . . anywhere. Alicia had left Hong Kong, her soldier family, her dead colleague and his upcoming funeral. She had left Matt Drake, the only man she believed might one day give her world and her life some kind of stability as he had before.

Leave the heartache behind, and find the horizon. What works today and worked yesterday will always work tomorrow.

Except, when it broke down.

Alicia shrugged it off for now, unhappy living with her own thoughts in her own head. The last thing she needed to hear was counsel from Alicia Myles. Focusing, she recalled that the plane was headed to the Southern US, which was where Crouch and his team had been. She had been planning a surprise visit; secretly hoping to catch Russo out and see his crestfallen face which she knew concealed a growing mutual respect. Now . . . she could land as planned and be on the next flight out. Maybe arriving not too far behind them.

Quickly she typed a message and hit send: *Landing in the US in one hour. Will advise time of arrival in Turkey.*

As she sat back, fixing her headphones to her ears and cranking the music up, she found her spirits lifted a little and hoped fervently that this was going to be one of those action-packed rollercoaster rides where the hits kept on coming, the treasure hunt never let up, and the enemies at least tried to put up a fight. The traumas in her head needed an outlet. Yes, she was ready to explode and even the mountain-like Russo would find it hard to withstand her eruption.

Here's to the adventure, she thought. *Never may it end.*

THREE

Crouch didn't relax until his team were on a plane and he'd heard from Alicia. A solid hour into their flight to Istanbul he called Sadler back.

"All right, Rolland. We're en route and ready to get to work."

"Good, good. Excellent job, Michael. As I said we're on the clock. Now, as I explained, many learned archaeologists are currently working night and day to excavate and explore the old docks. Imagine what secrets might be found there. Old crusader ships laden with gold. Spoils of war. Vestiges of medieval history. But even more. Constantinople's docks were international, of course, one of the busiest in those times. And Constantinople, with its infamous Hippodrome, its commerce and wealth and notoriety, not to mention one of history's greatest and largest churches—the Hagia Sophia— was the place to go. Ships from every part of the world docked there."

"And in particular a ship from Alexandria?" Crouch fathomed quickly.

Sadler laughed. "Of course. Are you all listening?"

Crouch looked around. Russo and Healey were busy picking through the airplane food with varying expressions of disgust. Caitlyn was looking introspective, perhaps dwelling on those events that had led her to this point in life. Crouch accepted that her input would be invaluable, but knew he'd hate himself if he interrupted her now.

"All as it should be," he said. "Carry on."

"So, after Rhacotis was renamed Alexandria by Alexander

the Great in roughly 331 BCE there followed the opening of the library and the lighthouse and then the besieging and the conquering and rebuilding from the likes of none less than Augustus, Julius Caesar and Hadrian. It suffered tsunamis, Persians, Byzantines and earthquakes. What stands today is built on tons of ruins. Imagine the constant peril of the treasures that have resided there. Imagine the dilemmas presented to those who ruled. Many times, it seems during those years, Alexandria's most important treasures were shipped out."

Crouch took a long drink from a bottle of water. "Perfectly understandable. With Alexandria's turbulent history I'd certainly want my valuables transported to a more stable location."

Sadler's voice quivered, perhaps with a little irony. "Well, Istanbul's lost Byzantine port has been discovered in a neighborhood of textile factories and shabby hotels. The docks silted over many years ago, vanishing beneath following civilizations, remembered only in ancient books. A truly stunning discovery, the excavators first found ropes and then entire ships—"

Russo snorted, now listening in. "So, back then they lost an entire ship?"

Sadler murmured a yes. "Thirty four of them to date," he said. "A truly fabulous, ancient armada."

Even Crouch was amazed by the story. "Any clues as to what they were carrying?"

"Oh yes. Wheat from Egypt. Pottery. All and sundry. And it is here where we find our new journey's first clue."

Caitlyn snapped out of her reverie. "Which is?"

"One of the ships they found was Alexandrian. And it seems it may have contained an astounding treasure."

Crouch's first impulse was not what but why. "And they sent it to Constantinople?"

"As I mentioned Alexandria was a seething cauldron of misfortune and catastrophe. Constantinople, by comparison, was a secure haven."

"Which treasure?" Russo rumbled.

"If I said to you the Hercules Tarentum what would you think?"

"Never heard of it."

"Or so you think. How about the Horses of St. Mark's? Or Lysippos?"

"Well, the Horses of St. Mark are in Venice. Everyone knows those. But Lyspy . . . os? Nope."

"Lysippos. Regarded as one of the greatest sculptors the world has ever known. He was the only sculptor Alexander the Great would allow to do his portrait. His second most famous work is Bucephalus, Alexander's horse. The ancient Romans knew all about Lysippos; he was written about time and time again and in particular by Pliny the Elder, one of the most famous Roman historians. In those times the market for Lysippos' work, real or fake, was as lively as any of your contemporary or renaissance artists today. Now, the real kicker is that out of a supposed 1500 bronze works not a single one has survived to this day. Not one."

"Are you saying that the Horses of St. Mark were sculpted by Lysippos?" Crouch wondered.

"Yes. It's the ears you see. Next time you feel like googling look at the close similarities between the Horses of St. Mark's and those of Bucephalus, Alexander's horse. At worst, the Horses are a copy, as are many others around the world to this day. Lysippos also set the classical tall, slim human standard in sculpting."

"I get it," Russo said. "The guy was good."

"Good?" Sadler echoed. "Understand this. His pupil, a man named Chares of Lindon constructed the Colossus of Rhodes, one of the Seven Wonders of the Ancient World."

"And what of the Hercules Tarentum?" Caitlyn asked.

"Ah, well the Horses and the Hercules have a peculiarly mixed history. Both born of Lysippos' talent, loved by Alexander, it is believed they possibly parted ways sometime after 323 BCE when Alexander died. Both works fell out of sight for many years, centuries in fact, reappearing in the palace of Nero, Emperor of Rome, for a short time and then the Horses at least were sent by Emperor Constantine to embellish the starting gates at his new Hippodrome in Constantinople. There they remained for almost a thousand years."

"And the Hercules?"

"Well, history is a bit fuzzier on that count. Yes, it was in Rome and Alexandria before that and believed to have been returned when Alexandria formally came under Roman jurisdiction in 80 BCE. Though linked to the Horses through circumstance and Lysippos himself, not much more was known about his greatest work—the Hercules Tarentum."

Crouch raised a brow. "Was?"

"The bill of lading as we know it now, originally called a bill of loading, is one of the most important documents in the history of shipping. It was invented, coincidentally and fortunately for us, in the thirteenth century. It was actually invented in Italy, because of the growing economy of sea commerce between Italian states and the Roman Empire in Constantinople. It formed a receipt of goods, contract of carriage, and a negotiable document of title."

"Do not tell me you found one intact?" Russo whistled.

"They did. Out of thirty four ships discovered, twenty had lock boxes wherein bills of lading and other items were found, fragile but intact. Archaeologists examined these documents in due course, and my contact, a man I shall call Naz, made the stunning discovery. On a bill of lading was an item described as 'The Tarentum Herakles.' The ship's hold was large enough to have transported the treasure, we believe. This find truly confirms that the Hercules was here, in Constantinople, with the Horses of St. Mark at the time of the Fourth Crusade."

"Sorry, you're losing me a little." Caitlyn spoke up. "Was there actually a dispute over the Hercules being there?"

"Yes. Many said it had been melted down before the thirteenth century for its vast bronze properties. But Naz believes the statue, one of a kind and quite possibly Lysippos' only surviving work of art, was hidden in the labyrinths underneath the Hagia Sophia when the crusaders came knocking, and quite possibly soon reunited with that other work of art—the Horses of St. Mark."

"Why?"

"I'll get to that. Or perhaps Naz will. But believe me—however famous and priceless the Horses are, the Hercules would top that with ease. The crusaders who destroyed Constantinople and many of its inhabitants during the Fourth Crusade stole many, many treasures, transporting them back to their homelands. That is how, of course, the Horses of St. Mark reside in Venice right now."

"Because the crusaders stole them?" Healey asked, munching on a bag of crisps.

"Stole. Plundered. But there are two sides to every coin. If it weren't for the Venetians taking them the Horses might well have been destroyed during those three fateful days like so many other irreplaceable treasures. Only the Venetians sought to save some of history's most remarkable creations."

"And yet it was their leader who led the attack," Crouch said carefully.

"You remember your history," Sadler said approvingly. "Yes, a man named Enrico Dandolo, the Doge of Venice."

"The man who had the Horses placed in Venice, atop St. Mark's Basilica."

"The very same."

"And this Hercules . . ." Russo said. "It would be valuable? A treasure for the world?"

"A true life's-best original of history's greatest ever sculptor and the only one of his works to survive almost two and a half thousand years of history? Oh yes."

"Fantastic." Russo nodded his enormous head. "When does this thing land?"

"Soon," Crouch said. "We need to hit the ground running. Secrets like this—they don't stay hidden for long."

Caitlyn glanced across. "Are we expecting trouble, sir?"

"I always expect trouble, Miss Nash. And Istanbul's a hotbed of iniquity. Rolland, does Naz know where the Hercules went?"

"Not exactly. But, being an archaeologist he does have a few ideas."

"We'll contact him once we get on the ground."

"Very good. And best of luck, Michael."

Crouch grinned. "No luck involved. We're the best at what we do."

FOUR

Alicia Myles heaved an internal sigh of relief as she felt the airplane's wheels touch down. Though never concerned about putting her life on the line she always preferred to do it on her own terms. A first-class soldier for most of her life, and now a renowned, accomplished operative, she had never settled, never stopped chasing that horizon. Her latest escapade as part of the SPEAR team had involved life threatening risk and daring head-to-heads in Japan and Hong Kong, ending with the mind-numbing death of one of their team—Komodo. Alicia would never forget the man or the growing certainty that if she didn't change the course of her life the rest of her days might well be measured in months, not years.

Istanbul was a sprawl of varied civilizations, the mingling of the ancient and the modern, teeming with the fanatical, the faithful and the indifferent. Alicia collected her carry-on and exited the plane amidst a steady stream of first-class passengers. Once through customs she sought out a cab and called Michael.

"Crouch? I've landed. Where are you?"

"We're outside the Hagia Sophia waiting for our tame archaeologist. It's a church, the largest—"

"I know what the bloody Hagia Sophia is," Alicia snapped, still a little wound up from the flight and its surprising turbulence. "Not just a stunner, y'know. At least I like to think so. Haven't had a real boyfriend to tell me in . . . well, forever."

Crouch clucked a little uncomfortably. "Okay. Grab a taxi and meet us here."

Alicia hung up, already buckled into the back seat. It would be good to see the Gold Team again. Despite herself she'd missed the belligerent but dependable Russo, the fresh-faced, talented Healey and the clever, mightily green newcomer—Caitlyn. She'd also missed Crouch's reassuring leadership skills and his sheer enthusiasm for anything even remotely related to ancient archaeology. That man had finally found his calling. Good for him. *One day my time will come.*

The streets were jam-packed with people and vehicles, dusty, sunbaked and yet the high roofs and towers rose above it all, shining, gleaming in the bright light as they stretched for the skies. Alicia kept her focus all around her, constantly on the lookout for any kind of conspirator, the soldier in her simply unable to switch off. When the great church appeared ahead she ignored its spectacular sprawl, its domes and minarets, its awe-inspiring edifice, and focused on the sidewalks all around, the gardens and any narrow alleyways. Such historical magnificence did not inspire her—it only served to remind her of all who had died in the name of religion.

Seeing her team up ahead, Alicia stopped the cab and paid the driver. Russo saw her first, swinging that enormous head like a lumbering prehistoric carnivore. Was that a smile on his lips or a slight grimace? Did he move to protect his extremities?

"Lovely," Alicia said as she came up to them. "A friend spots you in the crowd and then winces. How's it hanging, Robster?"

Russo winced again, this time more openly. "Just waiting for the bullets to start flying, Myles. They always seem to accompany you."

Alicia accepted a hug from Caitlyn and a smile from Healey. Crouch introduced the man he had been talking to.

"This is Naz. The man who brought Rolland in on the hunt.

Naz is an archaeologist and one of the men who's been risking his life on a daily basis to uncover the secrets of the old dock."

Naz grinned at her. "Yes. Tunneling is not my forte. Especially when I witnessed government soldiers bringing down a thirty-day food supply in case the tunnel they built collapsed."

Alicia shook her head. *No surprise there, mate.* Naz was a swarthy, lean individual with a thick beard and bright eyes. He wore a maroon T-shirt with holes around the neckline, dirty jeans and tattered trainers. The man looked more like a student playing at archaeology than a specialist.

"Where's your dad?" She looked around, shielding her eyes against the glaring sun.

Naz looked momentarily confused before catching Crouch's wry smile. "Oh, I see. Well, I am older than I look and very good at what I do. You will see."

"All I see is a great big piece of old rock. You wanna explain it to me?"

Naz turned toward the Hagia Sophia. "Oh really? There are countless books written about this old thing. My interest lies in what hasn't yet been found. The mysteries that still lie in wait for us, waiting to be uncovered."

"So why are we here?"

Naz glanced quickly at Crouch, as if gauging the newcomer's importance and her blunt persistence. "Well, we are here because this church has a significant impact on our quest. The secrets it possesses and has witnessed since its construction in 537 AD are limitless. It is the personification of Byzantine architecture, once referred to as 'changing the history of architecture'. Before the crusaders attacked in 1204 it contained numerous holy relics but then slowly began to fall into disrepair, then became a mosque and later a museum. This is what you see now. Of course, out of all that colorful history, I mention the crusader sack of 1204 for a particular reason."

Crouch nodded. "The Fourth Crusade was a turning point in history."

"Yes, and for many reasons. But for us, it marks the last known sighting of the treasure we seek—the Hercules Tarentum."

"Rolland mentioned that you found a bill of lading relating to the statue." Crouch remembered.

"Never heard of it." Alicia coughed.

"Yes, I found the bill. And to put it as succinctly as possible—the Hercules would be the only surviving piece sculpted by Alexander the Great's only sculptor, the same man who created the famed Horses of St. Mark and whose pupil built one of the ancient wonders of the world."

Alicia raised her eyebrows. "Gotcha."

"I thought it basically disappeared from the ship discovered at the ancient docks," Caitlyn said. "The history books said the Hercules was 'thought to have been hidden from the crusaders under Hagia Sophia'."

"No." Naz shook his head. "Many books from the *History of the Crusades* to Enrico Dandolo's *Attitude Toward Byzantium* make mention of the crusaders actually melting down the great statue for its content."

Crouch considered this carefully. "You mention Dandolo, as did Rolland. He was the only leader of the crusade who actively tried to prevent other crusaders from destroying the treasures."

"Exactly. It is what he did with the Horses of St. Mark, much of the interior of Hagia Sophia and countless other relics. Or so history tells us."

"So he saved them by stealing them?" Caitlyn said. "That doesn't exactly make him this city's great protector."

"Certainly not. Some believe Dandolo, once the Venetian ambassador to Constantinople, had his sights set on certain treasures long before the crusaders came knocking at

Constantinople's formidable door."

"Which might include the Hercules?" Caitlyn asked.

"It stands to reason. Dandolo led his Venetians in search of treasures. He did not take part in the destruction, desecration and murder of its inhabitants."

"All right," Crouch said. "So what makes you believe the statue wasn't melted down?"

"Beyond Dandolo's search? His deceptions? His obvious knowledge of the city? Just one thing—the Horses of St. Mark."

Crouch's gaze searched the middle-distance, wandering off in the direction of Istanbul's ancient Hippodrome. Today it was an intriguing city square with very few fragments of the original structure surviving, yet was still home to the pink granite Obelisk of Thutmose III, once erected at the Temple of Karnak in Luxor. It has survived nearly three thousand five hundred years of turmoil in remarkably good condition.

"Why do those Horses keep on cropping up?" Russo grumbled.

Naz smiled. "Because they are inextricably linked to the Hercules, mostly through their maker—Lysippos—but also by history and circumstance. It is no coincidence that both ended up in Constantinople at the same time, my new friends."

Alicia considered all she had learned and then spoke up. "Let me catch up. It shouldn't take too long. You found proof that this statue came to Constantinople, and then you called Rolland Sadler. Now we're here and we're all friends. Is that it?"

Naz grunted. "Well when you put it like that you take away the excitement and mystery of it all."

"Oh dear. I'm sorry. So what's next?" Alicia remained straight-faced.

"Hagia Sophia," Naz said. "You have to understand that, to

many, this church is as important as the Vatican. Tunnels twist underneath it that stretch all over Constantinople, and it was here that treasures were secreted during sieges. Until recently the Turkish government have never properly acknowledged that any tunnels exist beneath her. But then access was granted to a team of divers for just one day—"

"One day?" Crouch repeated, amazed.

"Yes. It's an odd government with an odd motive that would grant such a thing, don't you think? So we're left with thousands of years of speculation. People say that a cistern exists underneath her so large that a galley might sail through it."

"So the tunnels are flooded," Caitlyn reiterated.

"The ones we know about are," Naz said cryptically.

"So where does that leave us?" Crouch asked.

"Actually in a very interesting place . . ." Naz winked. "I would not bring you here without just and major cause. You see, the mystery deepens dramatically in this treasure hunt when you take into account the role of Enri—"

"Whoa!" Alicia suddenly exclaimed, eyes still surveying all perimeters. "Heads up, guys. There's some crazy-looking uber-bitch headed our way who I do not like the look of."

"Funny," Russo said, turning. "Those were my exact thoughts when you turned up."

The woman, Alicia saw, wore a bulky figure-concealing, knee-length coat even in such hot weather and was backed by a small force of gritty looking men, similarly attired. With dark hair and a dark complexion she might have been of local origin, or from anywhere east of Austria for that matter.

Alicia made ready, ignoring the ache of bruises that hadn't yet healed from her last battle, the pull of tendons overused. She had to be ready. It was her experience that violent conflict might strike at any time, from any angle and any person.

"Maybe she's lost and looking for directions," Naz ventured.

"She'll be heading straight down," Alicia murmured. "If she comes any closer."

The woman halted before them, a playful smile on her lips, eyes as cold as a natural predator locked onto those of its prey's.

Alicia recognized confidence, danger and death among other things. Her entire system instantly flooded with adrenalin.

"Hand over your archeologist," she said quietly. "If you want to live."

FIVE

Alicia was suddenly conscious of the many buses lining both sides of the road, the overhanging trees and small dome at her back, the swarms of people hailing from every culture all around. The new arrival patted her bulky coat at the hip and then motioned toward a nearby bus, the first in a never-ending line parked nose to tail.

"I'll gladly open fire," she said. "Makes no difference to me."

Alicia believed her. It wasn't the set of the face, the language of the body. It was those psycho eyes, void of all human emotion.

"We're unarmed," Healey said without thinking, probably trying to play the tourist card.

"Thanks for the confirmation, kid. Get behind the coach."

Alicia had already evaluated their position. Even counting Caitlyn and the archaeologist they were six versus nine. By no means insurmountable odds but highly risky without firearms.

Of course there were more ways to commandeer a gun than there were elitists staying at The Ritz. Alicia's calculating gaze swiveled between the woman's cohorts, determining the weakest of them.

Naz was the first to back away. "I do not know why you want me."

"Because he does." The woman shrugged in Crouch's direction. "I've had my hooks into you people since the Aztec affair. You liberated an awful lot of gold that day. An appetizing slice of money and wealth. I'm here for the main course."

"Clearly, you're deranged." Alicia moved to the woman's left ever so slowly. "Don't you have any idea who we are? What we could do to you?"

"Clearly, I don't care." The woman swept aside her coat to reveal a terrifying weapon—an Uzi Pro SMG; Israel Weapon Industries' latest design. Alicia knew it fired 9mm ammunition from the closed bolt and used the same blow-back operating system as the original Uzi design. Twenty-one inches long with stock fully extended and less than twelve inches in its most compact form, the Pro used a 25-round magazine and could be switched between semi- and fully-automatic fire. Here, among the tourists and the history, it was as deadly a weapon as the woman could ever have brought to bear.

Alicia hesitated. Were her goons sporting the same hardware? If so, the Gold Team's odds were falling by the second. Perhaps it was time for Plan B.

"So you're what? Another bloody stalker?" Alicia played for time. "Believe me, I've had more than my fair share of those recently."

"I bet. But you can call me Kenzie, and we'll have plenty of time to get to know each other during our treasure hunt, I'm sure. Though you might hate the chains."

"Oh, I don't know . . ."

"Now hurry up. I've already had to kill one of my men today and, despite his infinite ineptness, the death of a paid employee always festers in my gut." Kenzie spread her hands. "I mean, what happens to all that dead money in his bank account? Dead merc equals dead money and a waste of resources."

Alicia couldn't stop fleeting shadows of surprises sweeping her features.

"Yes, yes." Kenzie waved it away. "He failed me twice. I beat him, shot him in the gut, watched him bleed out. No fun in that. The coach is that way, blondie."

Alicia studied her adversary, not quite able to recall the last female criminal she or any of her teams had come up against. Was there one? To keep the woman happy she backed up a few steps, still with Russo and Healey at her side. Soldier's intuition told her they would be waiting for her move; an intuition not only born of expectation but also of mutual respect and experience gained from fighting together during the Aztec escapade. Naz already stood by the coach, Caitlyn and Crouch a meter to his left. Every second they stalled gave rise to the possibility that a distraction would present itself.

The driver of the lead coach leaned out of his half-open window, sleepily asking if he could help them out, and Alicia sensed the whole dynamic change. Kenzie's concentration shattered, leaving her irresolute for a short moment. Her men grew cautious, all of a sudden aware of how public they were.

Alicia had lived her life seizing the moment, and this one was no different. Striking hard, she bruised Kenzie's cheek, then sent her stumbling away with a jerk of her big coat.

Spinning past, she engaged her first crony, a man wearing a long leather jacket. His gun, secreted beneath, was instantly clasped between her hands and wrenched away. Above his shocked visage the extensive dome of Hagia Sophia loomed large, reminding her of their setting. Alicia doubled him over with a well-placed knee and threw his gun under the bus.

To her right and left Russo and Healey were backing her to the hilt. Russo smashed an elbow with the force of a boulder into one man's face, sending him into instant oblivion. Healey wrestled with a more competent foe, both men struggling for control of a weapon.

Alicia took another usurped Uzi and tucked in close to Kenzie. No one would dare fire on her now, even if they were mad enough to try out here. And these were not fanatical terrorists bent on destroying a larger world they had been brainwashed to hate; these were paid mercs intent on securing a larger pay day. Kenzie had said as much, betraying her hand. And though eyes now swiveled murderously in her direction all noted the presence of Kenzie mere inches away . . . and paused.

Russo threw a man against the side of the nearest coach, the impact itself turning a few heads. Healey slipped and scrambled away, pursued by his adversary. Crouch disappeared around the vehicle's blind side, drawing a contingent of mercenaries after him.

Alicia smashed a man on the bridge of the nose, watched him wobble before crashing to the ground, then rubbed the back of her spine against Kenzie's.

"Hey girlfriend. You ain't gonna shoot anyone out here. You've been outplayed."

Kenzie didn't move. "No. Not now. But I do see this treasure hunting game as a way of making money, far better than my previous drab existence of looting in the Middle East and fighting over a slab of ancient fucking rubble. And I will pursue you hard. Next time, you won't be so lucky."

"I don't need luck." Alicia pushed away from her, swiping another man as she spun. "I have skills. We were all well trained."

"And you think I wasn't?" Kenzie actually looked hurt. "The Mossad train the best, Alicia Myles. Remember that. And I was the cream of the crop."

Alicia noticed several passersby now staring, one man already tugging out a cellphone. "You need to get the hell out of here," she told Kenzie. "Before you're arrested by the Turkish police. You'll also be best served by forgetting you ever heard of our little team."

Kenzie snarled a little, eyes still set to frostbite. "You won't get rid of me that easily."

Alicia grinned happily. "Oh, I should hope the fuck not! We'll call this a skirmish. A fracas." She smashed a heel into Kenzie's midriff, sending her grunting backwards, then spun fast with a high kick that noisily cricked the tendons in a merc's neck. Holding onto the gun, she waded amongst the remaining men with Russo beside her.

"Don't hold back, will ya?" he muttered with mock anger.

"Not in my nature." Alicia fought hand-to-hand, jabbing, deflecting and reversing blows with two of Kenzie's men. Crouch came back around the side of the coach, struggling to fight off three adversaries with Caitlyn's help. The newcomer was being coached by Healey in their down time but still had a long, long way to go. Even as Alicia glanced over Caitlyn took a blow to the temple that staggered her. Healey noticed and almost yelped in anguish, tearing away from his current opponent to jump to her aid. Alicia gave chase, but found her way suddenly blocked by a returning Kenzie.

"Get you next time, Myles."

The Israeli sent a parting shot at Alicia's ribs, fast and arrow-straight and impossible to block. Alicia felt the impact, grimacing, knowing—as Kenzie had wanted her to—that here was a vicious, capable opponent. She exhaled carefully, ribs bruised.

"Only if you buy a set of muscles, bitch. I've had hugs that hurt more than that tap."

Kenzie struck again, not blinking, not conveying any kind of tell.

Alicia backed away this time, feeling the other woman's knuckles graze past her cheek. Now at her back she sensed another enemy, turned briefly and saw a tall bearded man reaching for her. As his fingers grabbed her throat she copied Kenzie's move of moments earlier—this time feeling the fracturing of bones.

"A lesson," she breathed and slipped away.

Kenzie barked an order, for the first time, it seemed, aware of the loitering passersby and the many visible cellphones. Her men rallied around, careful to conceal what weapons they still carried and started to slip away.

Alicia slipped to Crouch's side, inventorying their new cache and confident they had secured at least three Uzis. "So we're not going to be alone on our quest," she said.

"Never thought we would be." Crouch gave her a resigned smile. "If a legitimate search for buried treasure does one thing it always draws the rats from their burrows."

Caitlyn gasped a little as Healey applied a pack of tissues soaked in cold bottled water to the raw swelling on her temple. "At least she's not totally ruthless," the Englishwoman said. "And not totally competent."

Alicia stared after the already departed woman. "I'm reserving judgment," she said. "That little antic felt almost like a shot across the bows. An opening challenge. If she's as seasoned as she says she is and a veteran of the Middle East she'll be more than ruthless. But, hey, it could be worse."

Crouch grimaced as if recalling some of the worse enemies he'd come across in thirty years of soldiering. "Absolutely. We could have it much, much worse. Is everyone okay?"

The team spoke up. Even Naz joined in, wary but now looking much relieved. Alicia clapped him on the shoulder.

"So now you know what treasure hunting's all about, how about you get to the good stuff?"

SIX

Later that day the team checked into a Best Western at random, knowing a dogged enemy could still track them but still mindful not to make the task too easy. After the rooms were scanned and bags dumped the team met downstairs for drinks and snacks. Beyond the marble tiled lobby with its domed chandelier and highly polished paneling lay a compact rest area, complete with easy chairs and plush couches. The walls were covered in studded leather and the floors deeply carpeted. Drinks and canapés could be ordered from remote controls housed in the seats' armrests. Crouch shook his head at the advanced yet sterile technology.

"One more step away from human interaction," he said. "First texting, then scrolling mobiles and now a computer-controlled waitress."

"I like it," Caitlyn said. "Progress is not possible without change."

"Change is not always progress," Crouch countered. "As said Henry Ford."

"Didn't he design the Model T?"

"Yup. And he made sure you could order it in any color so long as that color was black."

The team settled unevenly, sprawling on the couches or throwing legs over the armchairs. Russo first waved Alicia away, but then good-naturedly cleared a pile of pillows to the side. Alicia gave him a sidelong glance.

"Chivalry is not dead."

"Oh it is. I just figure to put you between me and the lobby. Just in case your crazy friend finds us and takes a pot shot."

Alicia patted the hidden Uzi. "Kenzie? What? You don't like strong women?"

"Oh I love 'em. Just not with armies at their backs and a sackful of Uzis."

Crouch leaned toward them. "Whatever you think of her, this Kenzie person presents us with a unique problem. Our success has already spawned a complex conundrum. How does a specialized team hunt down ancient artifacts without attracting the attention of those who would destroy or steal or hold them for ransom? Truth be told it's not difficult to track anyone—even us—if you have the right tools."

"It's not like you can hop over to these places under the radar," Caitlyn said, playing with her hair. "They require investigation. Exploring."

"And quite often the cooperation of locals," Crouch said. "As you know I do have my contacts, but they're contacts built over many, many years. My guess is, even these men and women are not infallible."

"Don't worry," Alicia said. "Whether they're your contacts or not I still wouldn't trust them."

Crouch made a face as if he wasn't quite sure how to take that.

Naz also leaned forward, stealing their attention. "I was not done. When the crazy treasure seeker attacked I was not done. My thought process on learning that the Hercules had joined the Horses in Constantinople went straight to Enrico Dandolo, if you remember? As you now know he was the forty-second Doge of Venice and a particularly distinctive, exceptional man. Blinded in his sixties or seventies he then went on, at age ninety, to lead the Fourth Crusade and even later a foray against the Bulgarians. He died in 1205."

"The year after Constantinople was sacked," Crouch said.

"Yes. After successfully relocating the Horses of St. Mark from the quadriga atop the ancient Hippodrome to St. Mark's Basilica."

Caitlyn waited for the real-life waitress to deliver their drinks before speaking. "We all know where he stashed the Horses," she said with a wink. "But what did he do with the Hercules? Clearly, it wasn't in plain sight."

Naz nodded. "The one hundred—or much more—million dollar question. Was the statue a treasure so grand it was classified—assigned to be viewed only by the privileged? Was it deigned too valuable to show? Was it coveted, yearned for, perhaps beheld only by Dandolo himself? Hell, perhaps it was even forgotten. But I'll tell you one thing—" Naz paused for a drink, first making sure that all eyes were on him. "The clues to its whereabouts are all around us."

"Surely they need confirming." Caitlyn sat back.

"Yes, sure, and there is one easy way we can do that. I was ready to start today when the crazy woman attacked."

Crouch looked puzzled. "At the Hagia Sophia?"

"Yes, at the great church of Constantinople, where Dandolo himself once stood victorious. Do you know why?"

"Why don't ya tell us?" Alicia said soothingly.

"Dandolo's tomb. His body is inside the Hagia Sophia."

"No way!" Caitlyn exclaimed. "The tomb of the guy who led the crusaders into this city and practically destroyed it lies inside its greatest church?"

Naz nodded. "And that's where I was up to in my own investigation. About to visit the tomb, or more specifically the plaque of Enrico Dandolo to see what might be there."

Crouch closed his eyes. "I'm guessing the actual tomb no longer exists?"

Naz sighed. "Another mystery. His grave was encased in a marble tomb. Some say it was destroyed by the Ottoman Turks, others by the Niceans. And though the tomb may have been destroyed, the grave still exists."

"So what do we all do when we get there?" Alicia asked. "A polishing? If that's the case I sure ain't going near any bishops."

Naz sighed. "We investigate. I thought you people were treasure hunters. Isn't that what you do? Investigate? Follow clues?"

"We do." Caitlyn reached out to lay a reassuring hand atop the archaeologist's. "Alicia enjoys a little jokery."

"I'm not joking," Alicia confirmed, blonde hair whipping as she backed up her words with a nod of the head.

"Hey, I'll throw down some Jim to that." Russo suddenly held out his tumbler and knocked it against the feisty Englishwoman's. "No more joking around. Let's see how long that lasts."

"Interesting that you should do that," Crouch said, nodding at the tumblers. "The tapping together of glasses is a custom from medieval times and a sign of trust that your partner didn't slip you a deadly poison."

"Crap, that's fine," Alicia said, drinking. "So long as it doesn't mean I have to marry the lummox."

Russo sniffed. "See. Didn't last long."

"But I do trust you." Alicia held her glass in the air again, and this time everyone tapped it. "To the Hercules Tare . . . tar . . . crap. To Hercules and all his muscles."

"To Hercules," the group echoed.

Crouch settled back. "Is everyone up for an early treasure hunt inside the Hagia Sophia tomorrow morning?"

"Can't wait," Alicia said, slamming her empty glass down. "Wake me at dawn."

"It opens at nine. Tourist hours."

"Oh, all right then. Let's see if we can't figure out this armrest thingamajig and order us another round."

The buzz of alcohol did nothing to alleviate Alicia's pain. The power of the rain shower failed to howl down the voices in her head. Nothing could. She sat in her hotel room, at a work desk, wrapped in a towel from neck to toes, staring at a blank sheet of paper and trying to physically map out her future. It was an idea that had come to her late one night—sit there, think ahead, and try to write something down.

Anything.

Something that might prove to be an anchor. Seeing that, written down, might give her a goal to strive toward. It might turn on a light bulb inside her head, chasing the darkness away. There had never been a path, a plan. But without one she was doomed.

Get it written down, even if you throw the sheet of paper away afterwards it's still a start. A new start.

She picked up the pen, stamped a dot in the middle of the paper. A nucleus. It was a representation of herself, surrounded by nothing, heading nowhere. Life molded and changed you when you were young, events, sometimes menial, inexorably shaping you into the person you would become. Her own past involved a drunken father and a weak mother, both dead before she was twenty and forming the root of her problem and the reason she had started on this path. She was strong because her mother had been weak. She had lived through those days and would never take that from a man. Was it so hard to change now?

I like the person I am. How many people can say that?

But did she? Staring at the sheet of paper, blank apart from an empty black circle, she wondered where to go. The first detail she made was a simply arrow, facing upward, pointing ahead. The future. Then backwards—the past. One was indeterminate, the other inescapable. If all of life's decisions were this hard how the hell did people ever get anything done? Did they just make it up as they went along? Did they?

Making plans was one thing. But life choices? That was entirely another. The room around her was so quiet she found it a little threatening. If she made just one decision tonight then that would be enough. Just one. Behind her the bed looked inviting, promising the restful slumber that never came. Tentatively she drew another line . . . this one aimed diagonally halfway between moving forward and standing still. A progressive sidestep. If a compromise existed that might help her future then that was it. The trouble was—how could she fit it into her real life? The Gold Team were moving ahead, now engaged on another treasure trail. The SPEAR team never stopped—every day seemed to bring a new adventure for them. Was there a way to sidestep and still be a part of both crews? Because stopping was never going to be an option.

Life was too short.

One life . . . live it. Don't fuck around, just get involved and live it.

People died all the time. Good people. Not terrorists or asshole fanatics or corrupt figureheads or depraved gang members. Not sex traffickers or drug makers or gun runners or mass killers.

The good people died all the time. Innocent lives were lost every minute from the north to the south and the east to the west. If there was something inside Alicia that spoke truly it was a desire to help the good people of the world. This was what had changed her path long ago, from following the side of evil and switching to the side of good. No compromise.

Her eyes followed the new line—just a thin, inked arrow on a white sheet of paper—and wondered if it might change the course of her life.

Even save her life.

The question was—which name was waiting to be written above the arrow?

SEVEN

Caitlyn Nash tried to suppress her excitement as the entire team stepped into the hallowed interior of Hagia Sophia. This current structure, she knew, was in fact the third basilica built on this site, the first and second burned down. Of the first church, inaugurated in 360 AD, nothing now remained, but several large blocks of the second church, 415 AD, could still be sought out—among them blocks depicting twelve lambs for twelve apostles and discovered only seventy years ago. Who knew what other treasures existed inside this place and indeed around the world?

As they wandered the vast interior, Caitlyn again tried to rein in her awe. The nave was covered by the grand dome, almost two hundred feet high and resting on forty arched windows. To the east and west were other half domes and its interior was sheathed with gold mosaics and polychrome marbles. Caitlyn stopped in her tracks apparently to allow a group of tourists clear passage, but her wandering gaze betrayed her wonder.

Naz chuckled at her side. "Do not even try to take it all in. You will never move again."

Caitlyn blinked and then turned a quick gaze upon Crouch. Her boss was equally starstruck and the two gave a self-conscious laugh.

"Geeks," Alicia muttered. "Where to, Naz? Lead the way. I'm never comfortable inside a church for too long."

Russo practically barked. "Ha ha. I wonder why."

Caitlyn forced her legs forward as Naz led the way deeper inside. Though the hour was yet early the church was already crowded, jam-packed with camera-touting holiday makers, as noisy and busy as anywhere in Europe. Caitlyn fell in with the team, ignoring everything else, and tried to adapt as well as she could, still conscious of her inexperience, her naivety with most things military and the sharp learning curve that lay ahead. Back at MI5 the future had been assured, the present mapped out . . . structure and regulations put in place to help keep her secure. Those who conformed and listened and remained shrewd but undemanding were what they wanted. They didn't want James Bond. Caitlyn could have conformed until the cows came home and the heavens collapsed if all had remained stable in her personal life. Even a hiccup could have been ridden out.

But what happened between her parents was far beyond a hiccup. It was the worst unimaginable upheaval. Life stopped having meaning for her right then; the connotations of it tugged at her all the time, even now as she walked with new colleagues through this magnificent structure. How on earth could she not have known what was happening?

Ahead, Naz slowed, waiting for a knot of people to disperse. Once their constant chatter had died away he beckoned the team over, motioning at them to gather around.

"And here lies the tomb of Enrico Dandolo, leader of the Fourth Crusade and the man responsible for the sack of Constantinople."

Caitlyn looked at the ground. A simple plaque, a grave-marker bearing the name 'Henricus Dandolo', laid between rough borders of cement, lay humbly before them, protected by a simple rope and pedestal barrier. The marble floor all around it was cracked and worn as if parts had been uplifted or intentionally broken at some point in history.

"Somewhat unassuming," Crouch noted. "This is Dandolo's tomb?"

"Yes, or once was. Stories abound on this point as much as

they do with most of history's accuracies. Some say his bones were later dug up and scattered, possibly destroyed. Some say the Ottomans later desecrated his tomb. Some even say his body was quickly removed in anticipation of what may happen later. None of this matters. All we need to know is that once this was Dandolo's tomb and it was put here, inside this church, for a reason known only to him."

Caitlyn didn't take her eyes from the grimy-looking marker. "Why?"

"Because we're on a treasure hunt, Miss Nash," Crouch said. "And if Dandolo stole the Hercules along with the Horses and wanted the worthy to know about it, then he will have left us a clue. Don't forget, he ruled this place when he died."

Caitlyn searched the floor with her gaze. "Certainly there's no clue down there."

"No. He would have wanted it to remain forever," Naz said. "At least the life of the church."

"Which leaves us with . . ." Healey, close to Caitlyn's side, raised his head to take in the walls. The pale marble stone gave nothing away, jealously guarding its secrets now as it had for fifteen hundred years. Naz laughed.

"What did you expect? A poem? A map? A secret passage? The secret of the Hercules has lasted since 1204. Do not expect it to succumb so easily."

Caitlyn quickly scanned their surroundings, seeing nothing out of the ordinary. The team allowed another group of tourists to pass by, listening to their chatter of Dandolo and Istanbul, and then came together again.

"Do we know anything else of this man?" Caitlyn suggested. "Something that might give us a clue."

"Mostly what you have heard is all that is relevant," Naz said.

"Then we already know," Crouch said. "We already know the answer."

"But where . . ." Caitlyn turned full circle. Sunlight fell across the grave from one side, its bright shafts catching her eye. No way would that old trick work—a time of day and a shaft of light pointing a way to the ultimate treasure. A tourist with a camera lens almost as long as his arm leaned past her, shielding the light as he took a close-up snap of the tomb. Beyond him a darker doorway led to even more of the second-floor loge. Crouch backed away, affording more people a view and recognizing that the thing they needed would need more thought.

"Dandolo," he mused. "Constantinople. The Horses of St. Mark. Venice." He absorbed the display afforded by the tomb and its surrounds, the passageways leading off, the ceiling and the extensive floor. In truth the entire area was oddly bland, offering little in the way of mystery. Indeed, a wooden guard cabin stood behind them, inappropriate but probably necessary.

Crouch let his gaze wander.

Alicia and Russo, remaining distant, continued to guard the team's perimeter. Caitlyn entertained a moment of irrationality where she questioned the need for a guard inside this church, then again understood just how far she had to go to become a true team member.

Stupid girl.

"Ya see that statue?" Alicia was bantering with her large companion. "Bet you can't break it apart with your bare hands."

"Don't you ever shut up?"

"Only when I'm fighting."

Russo placed his hands together as if wishing for an adversary to turn up.

"Careful. You do that inside here too often they'll bronze you and stick you on a pedestal."

Caitlyn's attention wandered again, back to Crouch who

was staring into the middle-distance, then to Naz who was kneeling beyond the rope line, hands resting against Dandolo's grave marker as if it might be persuaded to reveal its innermost secrets. A beam of sunlight penetrated the clouds for a moment, filling the windows and glancing across the tomb.

The windows.

Crouch turned to her, his face alight, sunshine not the only glow lighting his features. "The windows!" he said.

EIGHT

Naz rose to face them, puzzled. "What are you talking about?"

Crouch grabbed the man's arm in his excitement. "The windows," he whispered. "Which set looks out onto the Hippodrome?"

"There is no Hippodrome anymore."

"I know. But in Dandolo's day. When the Horses of St. Mark surmounted it."

Naz looked like he'd experienced a sudden revelation. "Of course! The tomb was built here, in full view of the windows that stare out at the object of Constantinople that he coveted most, and stole." The archaeologist did a quick mental shuffle. "Those." He pointed and raced off.

"Slow down." Crouch caught him fast. "If anyone is watching . . ."

Naz's quick exuberance dissipated. "You mean the crazy woman?"

"Yes. And who knows what other trolls we may have picked up along the way."

"Trolls?" Naz's tone was confused.

"Trolls, yes. Those who seek to upset and destroy. From the one-star reviewers to the social media scavengers and nuisance hackers. Our intentions may be good, my friend, but that doesn't mean those we attract feel the same. So take it steady and look like a sightseer."

Gradually, the group gravitated over to the group of windows in question. As Caitlyn already knew they were made of stained glass and colorful—an arch of greens and blacks forming over individual panes tinted various hues of blue, red, white and green. As a whole each window was a simply stunning vision, but taken by individual panes and dissected, each one painted a different picture. Caitlyn counted eight separate panes to each window on the wall, which amounted to thirty two different scenes. Nonchalantly, but more carefully than she could have believed possible, she examined each one.

"Do you see it?" Healey muttered. "Anyone?"

"It would be easier if we knew what we were looking for," Naz admitted. "But I see nothing yet."

Caitlyn scanned the panes of glass, seeing dozens of religious images but nothing relevant. It took twenty minutes but eventually neither she nor Naz nor Crouch felt anything short of disappointment. The team knew they had already lingered a little too long.

"Back to the drawing board?" Alicia asked. "Well, one thing's for sure, all these failures will soon bore the arse off your bloody trolls."

It was then that Crouch's eye caught on a flash of color. "The Doge of Venice," he said carefully. "That could be it."

"What?" Naz asked, squinting toward the top row.

"A glass pane quietly dedicated to Dandolo near his tomb doesn't seem too out of place now does it?" Crouch murmured.

"Quietly?" Caitlyn questioned.

"It would have to be," Naz said. "Otherwise later generations would smash it. What are you seeing, Michael?"

"I'm thinking of the coat of arms of the Republic of Venice in Dandolo's day and the colors therein," Crouch said. "And I'm seeing them right at the very top there, dead center."

Naz inhaled swiftly. "Looking toward the Hippodrome, a pane of deep red and yellow with the lion symbol. That has to be it."

"But what does it portray?" Caitlyn squinted hard. "I can't

make out the figures."

Crouch removed his cellphone and held it up, focusing the lens but still blending perfectly with the hundreds of visitors all around. Taking his time he snapped several photos, careful not to stick to the same area. A few minutes later he was staring at the screen, blowing the most relevant picture up to full size as Caitlyn and Naz looked on.

"What do you see?" Alicia asked, curious despite her apparent indifferences.

"I see a male holding—" Crouch squinted. "Two items. I also see a miniature city perhaps? And, four horses. I definitely see four horses!"

"And the male," Naz breathed. "Look closer. Though small it is a man of strength holding up a key in one hand and a cup in the other. It is a depiction of the Hercules Tarentum. It is the statue as Lysippos sculpted it."

"And the city?" Healey asked.

"Where else?" Crouch smiled. "It is unmistakably Venice."

<u>*NINE*</u>

Alicia's elation was short-lived.

When Kenzie's now familiar face momentarily materialized out of the surrounding throng she knew their time inside the Hagia Sophia was up. She also knew that their new antagonist could not possibly be carrying any serious weapons. The entrances, halls and exits of the ancient church might appear antiquated but they were actually crammed full of the latest detection devices. Alicia signaled a hasty retreat and the team pulled together, drifting toward the nearest exit.

Kenzie must have caught on immediately, because she emerged from the crowd with her unattractive entourage. "I know you found something," she called across the busy space between them. "Just tell me what it was."

Alicia waved the others by, her and Russo trailing. Tourists milled all around. Within seconds Kenzie was tapping at Alicia's heels, leaning in to whisper into her ear. "Gloves are coming off real soon, bitch. You people are not going to know what hit you."

Alicia thought about all she had overcome and accomplished during the past few years and laughed. Kenzie's threat might not be an empty one but it was spoken with such outlandish bravado, such egotistical belief. Alicia's laugh only served to pour fuel onto the fire.

Kenzie slammed the bottom of her foot onto the back of Alicia's thigh, causing a jolt of flame to travel from the point of impact to her brain. Alicia pulled up abruptly, spinning to face the Israeli.

"You wanna eat the floor, sweetheart? Just say the word

and I'll put you down in front of all these people and their cameras."

"Put me down then, bitch. If you—"

"Amen, motherfucker." Alicia struck before the woman completed her sentence, a jab to the solar plexus and the throat. The first struck true, the second was deflected even as Kenzie doubled over, a sign that proved she'd at least gone through intensive training. Alicia stepped back, then brought a knee into Kenzie's head as her backup moved in.

At any other time, in any other place, soldiers and mercenaries might have backed off, remembered where they were and what they were doing. But not today. A challenge had been thrown down and nobody was prepared to yield.

Healey found himself barged backwards, fell down a step and realized he was at the top of a winding flight of stairs. A boyish enthusiasm creased his face and when the next man attacked he stepped briskly aside, allowing his opponent to sprawl headlong down the punishing flight.

Russo sent a man crashing against the stone balcony, its height the only thing saving him from toppling over. Naz backed down slowly, fronted by Caitlyn and Crouch.

Alicia found her attention partly distracted by Caitlyn. During the last few months Healey had been quietly and carefully training the young girl in an effort to at least give her the basic skills to defend herself. The team, and especially Alicia, weren't expecting any miracles but at the same time they were all hopeful. Caitlyn had controlled herself very well during the last adventure when she'd been abducted but Alicia didn't want to be called on for another gung-ho rescue any time soon. She'd had enough of those after saving Mai bloody Kitano from the hands of the Yakuza.

Now, as Caitlyn was forced to shield both herself and Naz alongside Crouch, the twenty-one-year-old was moving admirably, cutting down her target area and shifting in sync with the boss. Again, she looked calm. Alicia, and certainly her new opponent, wouldn't now have guessed she had no real fighting or military experience. When her opponent feinted at Crouch and struck at Caitlyn she defended by stepping away and kicking to the knee. Not bad. With the man on his knees, though, Caitlyn should have stepped in fast for the incapacitating blow—finish 'em off, Alicia had told her, doesn't matter how or where. Just end their ability to do harm to you or anyone else. Preferably forever. Countless times on the TV and in films she had seen the hero or heroine leave a capable opponent groaning behind them as they ran.

In real life you finished them off.

Heads were already swiveling toward them. Alicia had watched Kenzie pick herself up, knowing she could have injured the woman badly as she did so but feeling it might be a somewhat sadistic act.

See. I'm growing.

An Alicia during the Bones of Odin campaign would have struck first and thought about the consequences later.

Kenzie rose to her feet, trying not to gasp. Alicia held out a hand. "You okay? Want me to find you a chair?"

"This isn't over. The time will come—"

"Save it. Makes you sound like a friggin' supervillain. I'm thinking Thanos, especially with that massive forehead of yours. And the craziness. You can get tablets for that. So I'm told."

"One day."

"It's a bad girl's world, sweetie, and I'm way badder than you."

Kenzie held up a hand, forcing her men to back off. Too many heads were aimed their way, too many eyes and ears focused.

Alicia watched the play of emotions across the woman's features. Then, carefully, she also backed up, taking her team with her down the long staircase. The two units separated. Alicia headed for the nearest exit, already wondering how they could make a quick, clean escape. Crouch was a step ahead of her.

A door yawned to her left, already open.

The team surged through, hearing no shouts from the guards and taking it as a sign of good fortune. Outside, a bright sun flooded the day. Crouch held up his camera as he ran.

"We know where we're going. They don't. Let's make sure we leave them in Istanbul, guys."

Soon they were headed away from the church, a tree-lined path marking their progress toward a large contingent of cabs. Alicia and Russo guarded their every step, mindful of followers. Alicia thought she spotted Kenzie once, standing far away upon the basilica's steps, an expression of rage on her face.

Best place for you. Far away from me. You really have no idea . . .

And then, unexpectedly, Michael Crouch stopped.

The breath fell out of his body. The color washed right out of his face. Alicia saw it happen in an instant, saw the terrible, devastating shock attack his body and followed his gaze.

Heard his voice edged with terror, a sound so alien to him, so out of character.

"R . . . Riley?"

An older man faced them, probably in his early fifties, with the hard weathered face of someone who had seen too much, and fought too much. Well built, tall, and closely shaven from his chin to his scalp there was no mistaking that this man was or had been a soldier, and a very good one in his time.

And maybe still.

Crouch still continued to stammer. Alicia saw the rest of the team pause, unsure what to do, and knew the only action required now was to move forward. Nothing else mattered.

"You're in our way, bozo," she said.

The man switched his unreadable gaze toward her.

"Alicia Myles," he said. "I know you. And I heard you had changed. Why would you join forces with this killer? This criminal?"

It took Alicia a moment of staring from left to right to realize the newcomer was referring to her boss.

And Michael Crouch looked terrified.

TEN

Crouch finally found his tongue.

"Me? You have to be joking! There has never been a killer like you, Riley. At least not one I've ever come across."

Riley's stern face twitched with what might have been satisfaction. Alicia studied him, already shocked at Crouch's words and wondering why she'd never heard of the new dude. His hair was short-cropped, military style, and he held himself with a confident ease, portraying power, poise and intense training. Probably around fifty, he appeared fitter than most of the men at his back, young mercenaries all. But it was his gaze that held Alicia's attention—not just the frozen apocalyptic glare of his eyes but the wintry madness that shone forth, the controlled craziness that promised mercy would never enter the equation and bystanders were always accepted collateral.

"You thought I was dead?" Riley growled.

"I hoped you were dead."

Nobody moved. Tourists meandered around them, unconsciously giving the group a wide berth, perhaps sensing the intense, barely coiled violence that might erupt at any moment. Alicia noticed the arrival of Kenzie and her crew, and saw the woman's sudden realization that something huge was occurring here and to interrupt might cost a whole bunch of people their lives.

"When I found out you had turned treasure hunter I started tracking you down. Yeah, it took a while, but good things always come to . . . you know the rest. Found you briefly in Vegas, lost you during that Niagara Falls thing—"

"And now you're making your move?"

Riley gave Crouch an incredulous look. "My move? Do you really think this is my move? That you or any of your cretinous crew would still be alive? Believe this, Crouch, when I make my move you will be the first to know."

"So go fuck off then," Alicia couldn't help but say, bristling over being referred to as "cretinous". "Come back when you've grown a pair."

Kenzie drifted to within hearing distance, but well behind Russo, mostly hidden by the giant.

Riley sent that insane look toward Alicia. "This is the beginning," he said. "Your warning. Make no mistake, you're all already dead whether you leave this bastard's side or not, but I'll take it easier on you if you do. You're not under protection of the British Army anymore, Crouch. You're in the bigger world now. You're in my world."

"Always have been," Crouch said, but without true conviction. "I've always been around."

Riley blinked. "We'll see how different it is now. You of all people should know—I make the rules."

"Look," Alicia saw the already deadly anger between the pair starting to escalate to a point where it might become unstable, "let's save the testosterone. Looks like you boys're gonna need it later, not exactly being spring chickens and all. Riley—you ain't gonna try anything here among all these people so just back the fuck off."

Riley again transfixed her. "Believe me, Myles. These people, their lives, their children, mean nothing to me. I'd just as soon see them all blown into dust. This is all about Crouch, and watching him shit himself in the street. This is all about what's to come. This is to heighten the anticipation. Because when it happens—it'll go big."

Alicia searched Riley's face as he spoke, seeing only truth and disaster there, not a scrap of bravado. Suddenly the quest for Dandolo and Lysippos, Venice and the Hercules Tarentum seemed very far away. Devastation had just arrived on their doorstep.

"How come I've never heard of you?"

Riley blinked for the second time. "I am this man's nemesis. His dirty great secret. You think a big shot like Crouch ever lets the most terrifying skeletons escape from his closet? Well, this one just did. Ask him all about me. How we trained together. Marched together. Drank together. Ask him how he killed others just to try to get close and kill me. But the gloves are off now, as they say, and I will wage a vendetta, a bloody war, to destroy him and all that he loves."

Crouch didn't move, although all around him shifted to give themselves space. Alicia took in her surroundings without moving her head. "Bit over the top, dude."

For the first time Riley showed a trace of emotion in his face. A dreadful expression of hate distorted every feature.

"I will destroy entire cities to kill him if I have to, Myles. The game, the chase, is on. Take this as your warning before Armageddon."

And then, without the slightest hint of an order being passed, Riley and his entire team backed carefully away, expertly assessing their perimeter and withdrawal as they went. Alicia watched them a while and then turned to Crouch, a look of incredulity on her face.

"What in the name of the Downstairs DJ was all that about?"

ELEVEN

Bridget McKenzie stalked back to the vehicle that would return her to her headquarters, beaten and abused but only by conflicting emotions. Her plan had been one of intimidation, in true stalker fashion. Start low-key, build up steadily to the real violence—it all preyed on the victim's mind so much deeper that way, took them down quicker. And, of course, helped preserve her anonymity from the authorities.

What now?

Never, in her seven years as a dangerous rogue sinner had she had to confront a situation like the last one. This Riley had shaken her, surprised her with his intentions, the sheer animosity that radiated from him. Crouch appeared visibly shaken and though she knew him very little, Kenzie did know that the ex-leader of the Ninth Division was as battle-hardened and experienced as any soldier she had ever known.

Ex-Mossad, Kenzie had once been considered the best of the best. Israeli intelligence agents were highly trained, capable of feats even regiments like the SAS admired. The incident that turned her against them and against authority in general, and those that led up to it, changed her forever—giving her a belly full of anger, a burning mission, and a new desire to garner immoral power of her own.

The men who surrounded her now were mere guns for hire, or at least the majority of them were. One thing she knew about power—once you'd bought and fought for it you needed a few hand-picked individuals to help you keep it. Her inner circle was comprised of four strong men she trusted almost as much as she trusted herself. Beyond that she saw her men as an unruly tribe, a paid-for gang of thugs who might just as easily turn on her as follow her orders. With that thought in mind she carefully watched them, spied on them, bugged them, even paid outsiders to come in and pretend to be one of them, just so they could report all the heated conversations and secret intimations straight to her.

She trusted no one.

Not anymore.

With her plans for Crouch and Co. upset she settled back for a short drive and, upon arriving outside a dilapidated abandoned warehouse, slipped out of the car. With a look she summoned Ajax, a powerful, bearded American and part of her inner circle.

"What's your move, Kenzie?" he asked immediately, thinking how she expected him to think.

"For now we take stock," she replied as she walked, long legs eating up the ground. "This Riley's appearance is unexpected to say the very least and, judging by his extremist views toward Crouch, I'd say we really should re-evaluate our coming moves."

Ajax gave her a sidelong glance which she interpreted perfectly.

"No, I'm not afraid so don't presume to wonder. There is a reason I am in charge. Just carry out your orders and you will be fine."

"Sure. And they are?"

"First, a little diversion for me." Kenzie strode through the door, knowing Ajax wouldn't open it for her and not expecting him to. The warehouse's interior was sparse and grimy, just a vast cavern full of beaten, rusted relics that almost everyone had forgotten. Kenzie dealt mostly in the Middle East: stealing and trading ancient artifacts for money; murdering, extorting and torturing to find and authenticate them; then passing them through a tight organization she had helped create. Ancient relics were easy money, a tranquil and stress-free business compared to passing stolen Da Vincis and blood diamonds along. That meant she travelled often and didn't need an established HQ.

She cast an eye through the warehouse, saw her men gathered near an alcove to the side where an old refrigerator and kettle had been plugged in. A battered outdoor patio set lay to the side, the sturdier pieces now being utilized. The main warehouse area was an untidy clutter of ancient car parts, piles of worn-out tires, corroded wings and grilles and even a rusty old hoist. Pigeons nested in the spaces above, cooing softly. Motes of dust drifted lazily through the air. Her men were into the ale already, in particular those who had taken knocks from Alicia's crew.

"Lesson time." She spoke quietly, heading through the chaos toward them. "Make sure Gable, Hawke and Stefanov are with us."

Ajax motioned immediately to the remainder of her inner circle, knowing they had already been watching. Kenzie strode without fear among the rest of her crew, eighteen strong.

"An interesting time, gentlemen. A new player and one even I wasn't aware of. Still, it changes nothing. Just a single one of Crouch's treasure troves would set us up for life. And with that said, I want more men." Her affirmative gaze flicked briefly to Ajax. "A far stronger crew. See to it."

Ajax nodded.

Kenzie made a face, now including all her men in her gaze, effecting a confused expression. "So. With all these riches at hand do you think I'm leading you all wrong? Astray? Think I'm a rabid dog in need of putting down? Do you?"

Some of the older members of her team sat more upright, knowing what was coming. The newer members mostly copied Kenzie's own mien—looking confused. Some glanced between themselves.

"Ah, I can understand a little insubordination." Kenzie took out a thin blade and drew a thumb down its length. "I encourage it actually. Gets rid of that ridiculous testosterone. But there's a line." She held the thumb in the air, blood dripping along a red stripe. "You cross it you get to see my bloody side . . ."

Kenzie paused, gauging the reactions. Deep down, she was conscious that she was wasting time. She would be much better served by finding out what Crouch had been up to in that church and what the hell went down in the street afterwards. Her men had taken pictures of the window Crouch had seemed primarily interested in but they hadn't had time to study it. What were they looking for? The Gold Team—as they called themselves—were clever. Surveillance had turned up nothing, and had been scratchy at best. Every moment she wasted with her motley crew further worsened her chances of catching up to them.

Still, it needed to be done.

"During the last job," she said quietly. "Somebody gave away our position at the last minute."

All the men sat upright.

"I know." She acknowledged them. "Goes to what I always say. You just can't trust a mercenary or a criminal. Or anyone, actually. And that," she flicked her thumb rapidly, spraying blood across the floor, "is how I always know who done me fucking wrong."

With a leap she was among the men, touching no one, but springing from chair to chair, lethal blade twirling around her open hand. Within eighteen seconds she was done, standing behind them now on the opposite side, breathing slowly and smiling slightly.

The men blinked and looked shocked, uncertain what had happened.

Then, one of them toppled from his seat; somehow dead, somehow unable to voice his agony or even move until that moment of expiration.

Kenzie wiped her blade off on a piece of rag she found on the warehouse floor. "The lesson ends," she said. "Don't ever try to cross me. Bitch about me all you want, I like that. But plot against me and I'll stick a stiletto through your eyeball and into your brain. Or I may use the katana. My choice."

The men were quiet, staring mostly at the facedown man and the thin trickle of blood that had begun to leak across the floor, doubtlessly from one of his eyes or maybe both. Kenzie knew from experience that what shocked and disturbed them most was not that she had killed one of them as they watched—it was that they had been watching and hadn't seen her do it. The fact and the fear remained lodged inside their heads that it could have been any of them.

"Lesson learned?" Kenzie asked the rhetorical question. "I have eyes and ears among you. And I will weed out the traitors. And if it's you, you will die badly. Ajax—"

She turned to her right-hand man.

"The pictures?" He was smiling.

"The pictures."

Kenzie turned her back on her men, allowing them time to digest and re-evaluate. There was nothing like a show of deadly violence to rally a disparate team of mercs. Nothing she knew of anyway.

Ajax hooked up a laptop to his smart phone and brought up the pictures in question. The stained glass window with the silhouetted images of Crouch and others studying it filled the fifteen-inch screen. Kenzie flicked between them for a while, zeroing in on various parts, and then asked Stefanov to link his own smart phone to the same laptop. One of the only reasons she had so far kept in the background, limiting her actions mostly to surveillance and fisticuffs, was to allow

Crouch and Co. to find the treasure first. It was all a part of her plan. You don't take an art thief down before he steals the *Mona Lisa*. You take him out on the Champs Élysées, or even more preferably make sure you're flying the plane on which he later makes his escape. It was the same with Crouch. Too much action and violence now would cause her problems she could ill afford. Problems that might stop her from later acquiring the treasure. By any means necessary.

Stefanov had been filming proceedings. Video replay would work better in this situation, she thought. It would give a better indication as to exactly where Crouch and his team were looking.

"Top row," Ajax finally ventured. "I think."

Kenzie kept her silence but tended to agree. The treasure seekers were definitely studying something in one of the top two rows. But that was eight different choices, and at least six of them were a mystery to her.

"Disappointing," she murmured.

Stefanov nodded beside her. "You want me to—"

"I want you to start an investigation. Find out who this new player—Riley—is. Everything about his past and future. Go now." She waited until Stefanov stalked away, not liking assumptions being put in her mouth. Then she turned to Hawke. "Go with him. And use every contact our submissive Ninth Division mercenary has."

Hawke looked inquisitive and this time she could understand the hesitation. One of her men was an ex-British military man and an unknown survivor of the devastation wrought on the Ninth Division's HQ. Demoralized, discontented and wanting more he had signed up recently to Kenzie's crew, further cementing her decision to tail Crouch.

"Go." Kenzie watched Hawke leave, knowing she could trust him to do her bidding but slightly saddened that even among her inner circle questions and mistrust remained.

Blessed and cursed with a perfect memory she had once been the brightest up-and-comer the Mossad ever had. Quick to learn, even faster to correct mistakes, respectful to her superiors and loyal to her government, Kenzie was a rising star. One of her instructors had called her "the complete trainable animal, unsullied from head to toe". At first pleased and later highly confused, it took her a long time to understand the depths to which he was referring. Competitors called her green, fresh, but it was more than that. The military structure was one she embraced and even loved. She loved authority, reveled in the order and directness of it. It gave her purpose, stability and true resolve.

Which was why it came as such a shock and affected her so deeply when they so utterly betrayed her.

Ajax tapped the laptop's screen. "The team," he said, indicating Crouch and Myles and the others she knew as Healey, Russo and Caitlyn. "They left a man behind."

Kenzie nodded and sucked blood from her thumb. "I know. Go get me that fucking archaeologist."

TWELVE

The Gold Team left Istanbul in a hurry, their haste fueled by Michael Crouch who walked and talked and helped make their travel plans like a deep sea diver who's suddenly realized he's being tracked back to the surface by a great white shark. Through the hustle and bustle of Istanbul's streets and the whirlwind packing at their hotel room, the chaos that was Ataturk Airport and their ferrying out to a private jet, Alicia remained calm, almost silent, giving Crouch the time he needed to better apprise his team of the impending threat.

Riley.

She wondered if this meant the treasure hunt was off. More importantly—would Crouch disband the team? She knew how his mind worked. Experienced, military trained soldiers or not he would think first about keeping them safe when the slaughterer they faced sought only him. In addition, there was the potential civilian collateral to consider. If Riley was actually the madman he appeared to be then moms and dads and children would not be allowed to stand in his way. Crouch needed time to assimilate all the specifics.

Once aboard the private jet, seated and knowing its destination was Venice, she cracked open a small bottle of water.

"We have less than two hours before we land." She faced Crouch. "Best start talking, boss."

Crouch sighed loudly as he made a point of addressing them all. "First, there's nothing underhand going on. Everything between Riley and I is a matter of record. The man's a certifiable maniac, born without a glimmer of conscience and perfectly capable of destroying half the world to get what he wants."

"Which is you," Alicia put in helpfully.

"Ah, yes. So it seems. I had hoped the bastard was stone cold dead."

Alicia didn't have to look for any animosity in Crouch's tone, it was there undisguised for all to hear. "I'm guessing he kept tabs on you from whatever cesspool he's been hiding in."

"Riley holds grudges like an elected official holds the purse strings. Very tightly and close to his heart. No doubt he has known my every movement for years."

"Why hasn't he tried to kill you before?" Russo wanted to know.

Alicia glared at the rough-edged soldier. "Steady on, Rambo."

Crouch reached for a miniature whiskey, one of half-a-dozen he had carefully placed in a line before him. "Riley is hands-on. Yes, he needs men to make an opportunity but he'll want to do this himself."

"So the big question," Caitlyn said. "Is why?"

"Riley was SAS." Crouch launched into the explanation as if from an often-revisited memory. "We trained together. He was good. We were good." Crouch shook his head. "I underestimated him badly. More than once. Riley excelled right up until the last week of training . . ." He knocked back a neat shot. "When he disappeared. Now that just doesn't happen, not when a man's training for the Regiment. I was twenty three at the time and my friend had just caused one of the great mysteries within the SAS. Riley simply vanished out of sight, the promising career gone, his entire life gone. Left behind."

"So what happened?" Russo asked.

Crouch spread his hands. "It's still unexplained."

Alicia tucked an errant strand of hair behind her ear. "I still don't get why he wants to kill you so . . . intensely."

"Well, that's because you don't know the whole story yet. Riley was essentially dead to us for five years. You wonder about someone for that long, believe me, the reasons and scenarios you come up with would make for a fantasy novel. It became so bad I used to revisit the places I knew he'd frequented, make a nuisance of myself at his old haunts. No way could I believe a man like Riley could just disappear off the face of the fucking earth." Crouch took a few moments and polished off a second miniature.

"Grief changes you," Caitlyn said matter-of-factly. "Turns you into a different person. There's no way you can be the person you were ever again."

Alicia found her glance flicking momentarily toward the young girl. Caitlyn had experienced an immense upheaval recently in her life, something that had affected her entire way of existing. Alicia had been meaning to broach the subject but, as usual, incident and adventure had taken her away.

Crouch continued. "Indeed. As for Daniel Riley, my fears were not only unjustified but hugely wayward. Riley turned up five years later as a ruthless criminal, a tyrant with his filthy little fingers into just about everything. Some said he'd used the British Army to get his training, with a plan in mind all along. Others said he'd been recruited along the way and later killed his boss to take his place. The myths around Riley are numerous and relentless. I tend to think he was always bad, which is why I always believe that I intensely underestimated him." Crouch shook his head, finishing the third whiskey. "It never happened again."

Alicia noted that an hour had passed since they departed Istanbul. Soon, they would be descending toward Venice's Marco Polo airport. "I'm guessing you two locked horns later?"

"The SAS were informed of Riley's re-emergence days after it happened, but didn't actually encounter him until 1997, some twelve years later. I was thirty five then and no longer a new recruit. I was a captain. Riley popped back up our radar simply because he'd gotten himself into a fix by meeting a client in a hotel lobby in India. This client was a notorious bomb maker, a known killer, and we were already on the scene, having no knowledge that Riley would be there. Seeing an opportunity I walked into the lobby, alone, to reason with them . . ."

Crouch felt himself growing distant, remembering the events of that day with a memory too clear, a conscience too bruised. It had been more than an awakening; beyond even a grueling rite of passage. As he entered a lobby packed with unwitting bystanders he thought about all that the reports said Riley had done. The murders. The tortures. The kidnappings. Deals with the Devil. It couldn't be true, not totally. Riley had to have some ulterior motive. Perhaps he was working for one of the more covert government agencies. Undercover. Perhaps Crouch could now find out the truth.

The first person he saw was the bomb maker—tall, wrapped in silk, and sporting a thick beard. Beady little flashing eyes that could have belonged to either a rodent or one of Dante's demons. Crouch knew instantly that this man's slaying days would end today. Then, almost against their will his eyes found Riley. Was it really him? Would he be recognizable? What if—

But Riley had already seen him. It was as if an arrow shot between them—its trail a burning streak lined with old memories, old promises and a thousand unanswered questions. The intensity was so strong it stopped Crouch in his tracks and made Riley lose concentration, suddenly ignoring his client. The bomb maker caught on and turned, more prone to jumpiness than a kangaroo in mating season.

Riley rose quickly, surveying the entire scene as Crouch watched. In the next second he reacted in contradiction of Crouch's expectations and smiled widely, waving the Captain over.

"Michael! Michael! So good to see you. How long's it been? Ten years?"

"More." Crouch, caught in the spotlight, walked over, now even more conscious of the many people milling all about. The bomb maker in particular would have a contingency plan and might even now have a finger close to the proverbial trigger.

"I wondered when we would meet again," Riley said, in a tone implying absolute truth.

"I thought you might be dead. Buried in a ditch. Abducted and never found. I searched for you for many years."

Riley clearly read and understood the pain and outrage in Crouch's voice. "I never asked anyone to mourn me."

"And what? You're a terrorist now?"

Riley laughed, turning toward the bomb maker. "You'll have to forgive my friend here. He's a member of the SAS and not quite the stylish diplomat."

The bomb maker took that as a sign to flee, hopping over the back of the chair and showing Crouch, for the first time, that he held a number of small tubes in his right hand. Crouch stared first at them and then back at Riley.

"What have you done? Can you not see all these people?"

"You just cost me fifteen mill, asswipe. Now you'll be shoveling the remains of tourists up whilst I escape in my plane."

Crouch lunged, shocked but unable to let it pass. "Did you sell him those bombs?"

"The mixing ingredients, yes." Riley laughed, not an ounce of morality evident. "Now get the fuck outta—"

Crouch smashed him on the bridge of the nose, breaking it,

then caught him under the chin. Riley flinched and grunted, shocked and reeling aside. Seeing that Riley left a small disc-like object on the low table, Crouch swept it out of reach. Riley stared at it.

"You don't know what you're doing, Michael."

"I know you let the Regiment down. Let the Army down. I trusted you. Believed in you. And this . . . this!" Crouch attacked again, unable to help himself, dealing a blow that audibly snapped Riley's jawbone. The ex-soldier buckled.

"Let . . . let them down?" he babbled, wincing from the new pain. "Get down on the floor, man, because I really want you to live through this. Live and prosper. Because one day . . . one day I'm going to make you pay."

Crouch took Riley's advice immediately, surprised as he reacted without thought. The explosion shook the lobby, sending chunks of debris through the air. The first noise Crouch heard an instant after the explosion was the bump next to him and then he set eyes on the first casualty.

A flight attendant, stopping in the city for the night, living and breathing and feeling but a moment ago, rendered a lifeless carcass through Riley's actions.

Crouch turned away from the blank stare and the blood flow, saw Riley standing at the far end of the devastated room.

"One day," Riley mouthed, making a gun of his hand and pulling the trigger. "One . . . fucking . . . day."

THIRTEEN

Alicia listened as Crouch told his tale, at first surprised to find Crouch had such a horrific nemesis in his past, but then remembering that in the end they were all just soldiers. Could any man who had seen combat say any different? Nemeses came in many different forms and for every person who lived their lives.

Riley, it seemed, had bided his time and remembered his promise to Crouch on finding out he'd left the Army. Anyone who held a grudge for that amount of time should be taken seriously, no matter their proclivities, but in the case of Riley the threat was a thousand times worse.

Caitlyn spoke into a sudden silence. "I'll start some research. If we can find out what Riley's been doing since '97 it might give us some kind of an advantage."

Crouch agreed. "Start with Interpol. Riley's base of operations has always been Eastern Europe."

Alicia considered Crouch's story carefully. It was an event she knew fleetingly through past chatter. "Seven civilians and three soldiers were killed that day."

Crouch nodded. "Three SAS soldiers. But Riley, he is the master of disappearance. We never got near him again."

"I have to ask." Healey looked like he was about to burst. "What's next? Do we abandon our search for the Hercules to concentrate on Riley? Is that what you're saying?"

Crouch blew out a long gust of air. "Ahhh, I don't know. Riley has to be dealt with. If we allow him to operate I guarantee you he will end us all, publicly, with the highest amount of civilian casualties he can accomplish. But as for the fate of the Hercules . . ."

"It can wait?" Alicia said.

"It has waited all these years. But when a particular ball gets rolling so, usually, does another. Take Kenzie for example, and anyone she might have told. There may well be others. Rolland Sadler has to seek various permissions from local authorities to allow us to seek these treasures out— special access and the like. Criminals get wind that something is afoot, or they pay to hear from those in the know. I can guarantee you now that from our actions so far at least a dozen outsiders know what we're up to."

"And it's what some of them might do to the Hercules that worries us," Caitlyn put in.

"So we swing both ways." Alicia cracked a smile. "I can handle that."

Russo shook his head. "It's a bit of an alien concept for the rest of us," he said. "How can we juggle two such erratic variables?"

"It's this simple," Crouch said. "Riley will find us wherever we go. So let's do what we have to do and make sure we're ready for him."

Russo accepted this logic by clamping his mouth shut. Alicia slapped his broad shoulders. "C'mon, Robster. Is it true that men can't multitask? Or can even a slow, witless old Neanderthal like you make it work?"

Russo shrugged her off, growling softly. Healey cast a long glance toward Caitlyn. Alicia thought about the obvious wisecrack but then decided to let the two lovebirds be. The pair hadn't had a lot of luck just yet.

Is that me growing again? Is it? What the . . .

A weight hovered just above her shoulders, a weight that if it settled could literally crush her into dust. It lowered by the day, occasionally by the hour. Only situations like the one she faced right now kept it in the air.

"And on to business," she said quickly, seeing Venice emerge out of the cloud cover below. The beautiful island city spread out, appearing through the right-hand window as the pilot banked and turned in. A series of curves and channels, densely packed dwellings and a huge bridge like an outstretched arm, it diverted her with its intense attractiveness. The others were also staring.

"The Hercules Tarentum, being the greatest work of the greatest sculptor, will become a free-for-all if we allow it," Crouch said. "The chase is now on, like it or not."

"Speaking of Lysippos," Caitlyn said. "In school and through later studies I always believed Michelangelo or possibly Bernini were the greatest sculptors who ever lived."

"Most famous, yes. I guess it's arguable, but Michelangelo will always be known for the Pieta and David, both of which he sculpted before he was thirty. Bernini is known for so many works of art, including the Apollo and Daphne and his own David, the Baroque answer to Michelangelo's Renaissance original. Now what do all these and so many more have in common?"

Caitlyn thought about it for a time. Finally, she said. "They all still exist."

Crouch slapped an open palm down onto the table. "Exactly. They exist. All we have from Lysippos are copies, fakes and remolds. But consider this—even the copied Horses of St. Mark have been worshipped for thousands of years, fought for, and considered among history's greatest works of art." He paused. "Copies."

"Add to that the Alexander the Great connection . . ."

"And the Colossus of Rhodes being made by his pupil."

"Can't hurt having an original ancient wonder on your pupil's resume."

"And to Lysippos' stature add Eros Stringing the Bow. Agias. Hermes of Atalanta. The Alexander statues, from which the man's very image is now taken for granted. Alexander's horse—Bucephalus."

"Okay." Alicia thought it wise to stop Crouch as Venice grew clearer through the window. "But all we know is that Dodo brought the Horses to Venice after he sacked Constantinople."

Crouch tried not to glare at her. "Dandolo," he said, "stole the Horses and placed them atop St. Mark's Basilica. And there they stand today. We must apply a well-educated guess that the Hercules was also brought here by Dandolo and secreted away. It has certainly never turned up anywhere else and, indeed, why wouldn't it have been here? Dandolo was the Doge of Venice, it was his city to command. Of course he brought the Hercules here."

"For himself?" Caitlyn ventured.

"Undoubtedly. But not exclusively. You remember he was blind? I believe this was merely the spoils of war for a mad, old and dying Venetian. A trophy. One-upmanship. The Bugatti Veyron of 1204. 'Here, take a gander at my Horses. They used to stand atop the Hippodrome, you know. Do you like them? Well, here, let me show you this little secret treasure...' "

Alicia laughed. "Did you read that in a book?"

"Probably."

"So where do you think he hid the Herc?" Alicia quipped.

"We're about to find out." Crouch said confidently. "But from here on in, guys, it's deadly. No slacking off. No breaks and definitely no free time—" He gave Alicia an odd look.

Alicia frowned. "If you're referring to my time with Beauregard I don't count that as exactly free. If you do then try bouncing—"

"Either way," Crouch interrupted. "Beauregard's not in Europe. Stay close, all of you. Watch each other's back like never before. We're about to land and when Riley hits he will do so with devastating effect."

Alicia nodded with the rest of them, suddenly out of breath, knocked off-kilter. She wondered if anyone else picked up on it. *How the hell does Michael know Beauregard's not in Europe?*

FOURTEEN

Saint Mark's Basilica is the most famous of all Venice's great churches, an outstanding illustration of Venetian-Byzantine architecture. Connected to the Doge's palace it was once the chapel of the Doge, and thus effortlessly accessible by him. Adorned by gold-ground mosaics and seen as the status of Venetian power it was also known as the Church of Gold.

Caitlyn read that it had been linked to Alexandria since 828 on its conception, so it was no surprise that the basilica continued to be associated with Alexandria's great lost treasures and figureheads like Lysippos. Its very construction stemmed from and was ordered after merchants from Venice stole the supposed relics of Mark the Evangelist from Alexandria. Belief and myths surround it, and wrap it in an air of mystery. The body of St. Mark was discovered inside a pillar by the then-ruling Doge. Part of it is said to be what is now left of the original Doge's palace. Countless adornments spring from the Fourth Crusade and the sack of Constantinople. Caitlyn immediately knew, on reading, what Crouch already supposed—that the Hercules Tarentum, if it were still in existence, would be here, behind these hallowed walls.

She already knew a little of the Horses themselves, how they dated back to Classical Antiquity, were thought to be a team originally pulling a quadriga chariot containing an emperor, and that the ones on display outside the church were fakes—the real ones now kept inside the church where the elements were far kinder to them.

Now, as the team crossed St. Mark's Square, hemmed by

snapping tourists at every step, surrounded by the ever-present pigeons, a light drizzle fell. Ahead stood the impressive basilica and, to its right, the three-hundred-foot-tall bell tower, one of Venice's most recognizable landmarks. The square opened out to the right, leading to one of the canals. Caitlyn concentrated on the church, already able to see the bronzed Horses standing in pride of place atop the arched entrance. Caitlyn counted five huge arches ahead, or portals, as they were referred to. Seeing the size of the structure she tapped Crouch on the shoulder.

"Now would be a good time to call one of your contacts."

Crouch nodded a little reluctantly. "I'd like to get a feel for the place first," he said. "Nose around a bit. But Riley and Kenzie and their threats mean we're running against the clock now. Trouble is, I have contacts in most countries, even Italy, but not with the Roman Catholic Church or the Patriarch of Venice."

"Can't we . . . you know," Russo mumbled. "Have a chat with him."

Crouch looked a little aghast. "The Patriarch is appointed by the Pope himself. No, Russo, we can't have a word with him."

Alicia sighed. "And there goes any chance of me being able to use my womanly wiles on him."

Russo choked with laughter. "Oh, yeah. Really? You have those?"

"Wait a minute," Caitlyn said, almost stepping on a pigeon. "I thought you said the basilica belonged to the Doge, not the local bishop."

"Used to." Crouch also had to wade through a knot of pecking birds. "I remember reading it changed over slowly, finally overseen by Napoleon during his years of control in Venice."

Caitlyn blinked at that. "Who? Napoleon? Of France? How did he—"

But at that moment, with the basilica before them, and the skies lightening up above to show a blanket of pure blue, Crouch's cellphone rang. To both sides tourists glanced across as if the tinny droning of a ringtone was in violation of the piazza's rules. Crouch answered.

"Yes?"

Caitlyn watched him as the others all checked their perimeter. Surveillance was everything now—it would keep them alive. Nobody trusted that even the sacrosanct piazza would blunt Riley's strike when it happened.

Crouch was silent, listening, but Caitlyn saw a world of hurt enter his eyes the second before he squeezed them tightly closed. His head fell. She knew something was terribly wrong.

She stepped forward. "Michael?"

Crouch whispered something into the handset. A stiff breeze, laced with the last vestiges of the shower, swept Caitlyn's hair aside. A darkness fell over Michael Crouch as the sun finally split the heavens that peered down upon the basilica.

"Michael?" she repeated. Alicia turned toward her, noting the urgent tone of her voice.

Crouch spoke again, his voice too low to understand. It didn't happen often, but when Caitlyn saw the fight go out of him in such a way it disturbed her on deeper level than she cared to admit.

He saved me. Gave me a second chance. Caitlyn had been in Hell when Crouch recruited her, wallowing, failing, drowning in grief. The subsequent weeks and months had helped her deal with the revelations surrounding her mother and father, but the horror of it all still clung and lurked like toxic shadows.

Alicia tapped her on the shoulder. "What's going on?"

"I don't know. He just answered his cell—"

Crouch ended his call, eyes still closed, face as tight as a photo finish. When he did finally look at them he did so under an immense strain.

"That was Interpol. The Istanbul police are reporting finding a body." He gripped the bridge of his nose between two fingers. "One of the city's esteemed archaeologists. Seems he was tortured for information and then killed."

Alicia stepped forward immediately. "Naz? You're saying . . ." she tailed off, seeing the same truth that Caitlyn saw in Crouch's chaotic gaze.

"I'm responsible," Crouch said. "I brought him into this. I left him alone, thinking everything would just move on—"

"How could you know Riley would go after him?" Healey asked. "You didn't kill him—"

"It wasn't Riley," Crouch said.

Now Alicia grunted. "Then who? Kenzie. Not Kenzie—"

"Police report CCTV cameras show her in the vicinity of the murder around the right time."

"Shit, did we underestimate her." It was a statement of fact.

"Yes, we did." Crouch let out a long breath. "She's as psychotic as bloody Riley and now she also knows where we were headed."

Russo continued to survey the area. "She ain't here yet, boss."

Caitlyn gestured toward the sheer amount of people crowded into the square. "You can't know that for sure."

Russo shrugged, a rock face convulsing.

Alicia pointed toward the basilica. "Keep moving. Standing in one place for too long is what gets you killed. Look, the Horses are right there, right in front of us. Bronze copies of the ones Lysippos sculpted. That's our link. Dandolo brought them here at the same time he brought the Hercules. So where is it?"

Her words took a moment to impinge upon Crouch, but

when they did he abruptly nodded. "You're right, Myles. We should get inside St. Marks."

He shoved past them all, now shouldering another burden. Alicia strode after him and Healey beckoned to Caitlyn.

"Hurry. We shouldn't be separated."

Russo appeared to be inspecting every face and feature within their vicinity. "They could be anywhere," he finally admitted. "And they won't hesitate. C'mon, guys. Get a bloody shift on."

Once inside, the interior of St. Mark's Basilica hit them like a warm blanket of gold. The shining yellow domes, the walls, the mosaics, all spoke of beauty, priceless art and wealth. It was laid out in the shape of a Greek cross, each arm divided into three naves with a dome of its own in addition to the main dome above the crossing.

Caitlyn was immediately stunned by the size of the place. "Wow, it's huge. How on earth do we even start a search?"

"We simply search," Crouch snapped. "Did you think it was going to be easy? Look for clues. For anything relating to what we know. To mosaics, murals, stained glass windows. To the Doge of the thirteenth century. To the horses. To Hercules. Lysippos, even. And Alexander. Use your bloody brain."

Caitlyn drew back as their boss stalked on ahead. Alicia kept pace for a moment. "Leave him be. Michael's been a leader longer than you've been mature. And do you know what a good leader's worst nightmare is?"

"Losing the respect of their people?" Caitlyn said sharply.

"No. But close. It's losing their people. Through no fault of his own Crouch lost the Ninth Division. Or did you truly think all this treasure hunt business was purely for fun?"

"You're saying he's using it to cope?"

Alicia stopped at the end of a long row of chairs. "Partially, yes. Whatever he says to the contrary. There's much more to him than meets the eye."

Caitlyn caught a tone of warning within Alicia's words and studied her more closely. "What's that supposed to mean?"

"He's deep. Deeper than even I knew. I'm not entirely sure yet but—" the Englishwoman clammed up, surprise in her eyes showing she probably hadn't even meant to say that much. Caitlyn knew she would get no more out of Alicia Myles.

"Well, keep me informed."

"Like an older car salesman. I always do when it suits me to."

Caitlyn slowed, conscious that she'd already crossed a good proportion of the lower register and taken in very little. Something struck her that had seemed a little odd when Crouch proposed it. Why would this church have any references to Hercules?

Unless . . .

It was an oddity, for sure, and one that required investigation. If St. Mark's Basilica bore any indications of Hercules it may well be a sign, a lead. Quickly, she sat down on one of the chairs and found her Kindle Fire, logging into a web browser. Healey stood over her, reminding her of the need for protection.

In here?

Terrorists, murderers and other fanatical or psychopathic killers would not stand on ceremony. Caitlyn watched Crouch passing between rows of pillars, studying the inlaid paving at his feet. Russo and Alicia studied a wall showing apostles, angels, a winged lion and St. Mark himself. Caitlyn thought hard. They already knew that at least one major work of Lysippos adorned this so-called cathedral church, but could there be any more?

The Four Tetrarchs statue stood inside, also robbed from Constantinople, as did many other objects. None of them helped. Most weren't even sculptures, but she reminded herself not to think in such a linear way. Clues might come in all shapes and sizes.

As Caitlyn tapped away, Alicia and Russo wandered the aisles, threading in and out of the great columns and always watching. Above, the other levels overlooked them and made it harder to guarantee safety, but the pair made the Gold Team as secure as they could. Crouch stood apart, wrestling with his idea that a clue must exist inside the basilica as much as the latest revelation about Naz's death. Their boss checked every statue, every mosaic, and came up with nothing.

More than an hour passed, the minutes ticking away. It was Caitlyn who finally made a breakthrough.

Studying page after page of information and retaining as much as she was able, she came across an article that amazed her. On reading she rose and waved to the entire crew, ignoring Crouch's look of anger that clearly shouted: Discretion!

"I've found something," she said, unable to keep a note of excitement out of her voice. "This façade," she pointed, "is split into two orders, all overlooked by the copy of the quadriga of St. Mark. The Horses. Now listen—'the *thirteenth century* marble facing . . .' " she clearly emphasized the date. " '. . . includes several sculpted Byzantine slabs. Two of them are portrayals of the Labors of Hercules. Hercules with the Boar of Erymanthus from the fifth century and another from the thirteenth century'." She paused, staring at Crouch.

"I like it," he said shortly. "In particular that the entire façade dates from after our Hercules probably arrived."

Caitlyn stood up. "We're all aware of our time limitations. Let's go."

The team reacted to her abrupt air, marching toward the façade she had pointed out. Crouch gave her a look as he turned, one of gratitude, which she also took as part apology.

Trouble was, she couldn't stay mad at her benefactor for long. He was just too well respected and had already helped her beyond measure.

The first sculpture they looked at depicted Hercules with the Hind of Cerynea and the Hydra of Lerna; the legendary figure grappling with and wrestling both. Alicia squinted hard.

"He's not wearing much is he? Doesn't look like Dwayne Johnson to me. Or Reece Carrera for that matter, our pet movie star. Not that I've ever seen either man's family jewels. Yet."

Caitlyn tilted her head. "Family jewels?"

Alicia laughed and glanced at Healey. "Are you two really that bloody young? How about beanbag? Knackers? Clappers?"

Russo leaned in, saving Caitlyn. "She means 'bollocks'."

Caitlyn caught on, then retorted in double-time. "She usually does."

Alicia grinned, studying the slab even harder. "So. What we have here is a half-naked dude in the middle of a fight—"

"His labors," Caitlyn put in.

"Yeah, whatever. But what you don't have is anything else. No background. No clues, love. Unless the Hydra or the Hind mean anything?"

"Third labor," Crouch recited from memory. "Instead of slaying monsters, which Herc had already proved he could do, they made him catch the Hind which was faster than an arrow." He thought about the reference. "He chased it for a year through Greece, Thrace, Istria and Hyperborea. It was a defiant moment for him. He eventually let the Hind go, alive. I see nothing in this carving that helps us."

Alicia turned away, the piece already forgotten. "And the other?"

"Hercules with the Boar of Erymanthus. The fourth labor.

Hercules captures the boar and returns it alive, but the tale is generally accepted to portray how Chiron surrendered his immortality to the great man. A tale of how the Centaurs died."

Crouch chewed his lip, considering the facts. Alicia studied the sculpture. This time, Hercules carried the huge boar over his shoulders and appeared to be threatening a man, his tormentor, with it. Again there were no other images to consider, no hidden words or depictions.

"They say pictures convey a thousand words," Alicia grunted. "Well, these sculptures "portray two, maybe three. And I am totally—"

"No swearing in church, Alicia," Russo said. "I'm sure you're already booked into Hell when you die so no need to make it worse."

"She's right though," Crouch looked around, disappointed. "Our best clues point to nothing. Nothing at all. Look people, we've been tramping around in here for hours now with nothing to show for it. How about we take a break?"

"With our competitors so close?" Russo asked.

"Better they hit us in a coffee shop than here." Crouch shrugged.

Caitlyn looked around the despondent crew. *We failed.* They had failed Naz, failed Sadler, failed themselves. "There's nothing upstairs?" she pressed. "Near the Horses?"

"It's all stone and marble," Crouch said. "No secret rooms that I can see. No disguised entrances. No floor marks where a statue might occasionally be dragged out on display for the privileged to view. We've by no means searched this entire place yet, but I'm also thinking that that's an impossible feat. My contacts have said they may be able to get us a night in here but even that may take some time to arrange."

Caitlyn fell in line as the group carefully and despondently exited the church. Nobody needed to mention their desperate need to conclude all this. Riley and Kenzie could be out there among the milling crowds, watching them even now. She actually thought Crouch's idea a sound one—they couldn't wander the halls and hope for the best. Somebody, one of them, had to come up with a plan, a breakthrough, a new development.

Were the Hercules sculptures adorning the façade really useless?

"Maybe it's in the legend," she said aloud. "The Labors. Maybe we should research them some more."

"We will," Crouch said. "But it could be any of the other balls we are juggling right now too. In particular, Dandolo. That clever old blind man knew exactly what he was doing as Doge of Venice and he most definitely won't have squandered such a magnificent treasure."

Caitlyn stopped in the piazza, casting a glance backward. The spirits of the famous Horses of St. Mark watched her, dripping in history, awash with memories of olden times. What secrets did they yet hold?

"Y'know," Alicia said at her side. "There are horses like that on top of the London Hippodrome too."

Caitlyn laughed. "Yes, I know, but not exactly steeped in so much history."

"I mention it only because most people don't look up. Most Londoners wandering Leicester Square don't realize the horses are there."

"And there," Crouch walked momentarily backwards, pointing even higher. "Stands St. Mark, flanked by six angels, above a large gilded winged lion. His symbol and the symbol of Venice."

"We get it," Russo said. "The dude's important."

"Yet another reason to believe the most important lost statue in history is right here." Crouch winked and led the way.

FIFTEEN

Alicia settled at the small round table with an iced Maple Macchiato in one hand. Their chosen table afforded them a clear view of the street outside, some ten minutes' walk from St. Mark's Square. The soldiers among them were feeling a little somnolent from all the sightseeing.

Alicia said as much. "I think I need more than a drink, guys. All this aimless walking makes me more tired than a rapid action battle."

"I have to agree." Crouch stretched his legs and looked drained. "Time for a break."

"So speaks the relentless tomb raider." Alicia smiled affectionately. "Your life's dream has been to inspect dusty old churches."

"In a manner of speaking—yes. Ancient treasure doesn't find itself. And it's not always easy. If it were there would be nothing left to find."

"Perhaps we should be looking from a different angle," Caitlyn speculated.

"It's not always there either. It's already been looted or destroyed," Healey spoke up. "Hence the reason most people don't bother looking."

"You saying we're on a wild goose chase?" Alicia pounced on the young man's intimations.

"I dunno. We were inside for three hours and have nothing beyond two boring old Hercules sculptures to show for it. Don't forget we have other problems on the way."

Alicia nodded, looking over to the food counter. Already Caitlyn and Crouch were tapping away on their tablets, comparing local information with what they already knew. Alicia sipped at her drink, enjoying the distinction between sweetness and ice, water and coffee. Russo, sat beside her, kept his gaze fixed on the picture window.

"No matter where we go," he said, "what we do. Our job, our deeds, always follow us."

"Because we're soldiers?" Alicia asked. "Or people?"

"Soldiers first. Always."

"So how do we stop running?"

Russo's gaze shimmered with alarm. He didn't move his head, but his next words were clearly carefully chosen. "We make the decision to. And stick by that decision no matter what happens."

"That's it?"

"Yup."

"You make it sound easy, Russo. I've been skirting that easiness my entire adult life."

"Myles," Russo shot a fast glance her way, "is anything with you ever easy? No. Expect the worse."

"Will do, Cap'n." She gave the soldier a mock salute and went back to nursing her macchiato. Crowds drifted past the finger-stained glass, many with cameras swinging from their necks or fingers. More tapped on cellphones as they walked, uncaring about who they agitated. Several sat or crouched against a far concrete wall, taking a break from the dog-eat-dog world of exploration. The crowds inside the coffee shop ebbed and waned, first full to standing room only and then emptying out before another onslaught. As the day wore on the masses thinned and the light faded. Crouch and Caitlyn gave up more than once.

"All right, here's another idea," Caitlyn said for the fourth time that hour. "How about we take it back to the beginning. Lysippos. Then Alexandria and Constantinople. What's our only other constant until then?"

Crouch shook his head. "I already mentioned this. It's the Horses, of course. The bloody, silly Horses."

"Calm down, boss," Russo rumbled. "Won't get anywhere with a grump on."

Alicia took her seat again at that point, having visited the food counter, and unwrapped a roast chicken sandwich.

Caitlyn nodded, eyeing the meal hungrily. "Yes, but beyond that we know nothing. Well, here's an interesting fact. They're one of the most often stolen and recovered treasures in history."

"What? Are you kidding? You mean they were stolen again? After Dandolo?"

"Well, for a brief period, yes. First stolen by Constantine, then Dandolo. And then once more—they were also stolen by Napoleon."

SIXTEEN

"Napoleon?" Crouch echoed. "Are you kidding? That means—"

Caitlyn nodded, interrupting in her eagerness. "Yes, they were taken from St. Mark's Basilica in 1797 and installed in Paris."

Russo turned with a raised eyebrow. "So how'd they get back here? Galloped, did they?"

"When Napoleon was defeated in 1815 the conquering allies returned them to Venice."

Alicia grunted. "Not Constantinople? I bet that irked."

"No doubt, but here they stand. And the good news is they've not been stolen since."

Crouch looked over at her. "Are you suggesting that Napoleon, enamored enough to dismantle and remove the Horses, might also have found the Hercules and stolen that too?"

"Why not? If he knew the provenance of one he'd have known the other. If the Hercules was hidden he'd have grasped its importance pretty quick. He spent time in Venice and he was a bona fide conquering hero like Dandolo and the Roman Emperors before him."

"But we have no proof," Crouch stressed. "The trail is still cold. What we need to find is something tangible."

"Well, history states that Napoleon captured Venice and took plunder. He kept the Horses for eighteen years until Wellington defeated him. France then ceded the Horses back to the Venetians. So, did Napoleon originally keep the statue for his private collection as Dandolo no doubt did?"

"That's not proof," Healey pointed out.

"No, but the statue has now hit its own quiet point in history. The trail is cold. We have to somehow prove Napoleon took it to Paris."

Crouch rose and wandered over to the food counter as Alicia finished her sandwich. "Hate to say this, guys," she said. "But you're grasping now."

Caitlyn shrugged. "Hey, we failed at the basilica. Where else do we go from here?"

"Their reasoning is true," Russo said unexpectedly. "It must have cost Napoleon enormous effort to remove those Horses. He would have taken the superior treasure too."

Alicia spotted the man moving toward Crouch immediately. She rose quickly even as Crouch wheeled toward him, and then they both paused.

"Ah." Alicia said. "This could be awkward."

Crouch smiled as the man approached.

"Beware of false prophets," he said.

Crouch nodded. "Always am. Thanks." And turned away.

The man pointed to the board that hung around his neck. *I am the way, the truth, and the life,* it said. The words of Jesus Christ.

Alicia had no problem with religious views so long as they stayed below the level of fanatical. She nodded at Caitlyn to pass Crouch's tablet across. "I think the boss is gonna be a while."

"Beware of false prophets," the man reiterated, turning to address the entire café now. "Which come to you in sheep's clothing, but inwardly they are ravening wolves."

Alicia knitted her brows. Russo glanced away from the window. "Is he talking about us?"

"Why, Rob? Are you false?" Alicia's comment was off-the-cuff, because she was actually thinking about Crouch and his previous statement concerning Beauregard. False prophet?

Never.

Russo tapped the table, drawing the man's attention. "The only thing necessary for evil to triumph is for good men to do nothing."

"Good quote," Alicia said, wondering if there was more to Russo than she had previously thought.

"Old quote," Russo said. "Not mine. And one of the best."

Crouch turned to them just as the man grinned; just as the café door swung open so violently its glass smashed; just as windows on all sides shattered; just as all hell broke loose in the city of heaven.

War had come to Venice.

SEVENTEEN

Alicia reacted with pure animal instinct. As a razor-edged waterfall rained down to her left, she upended the table and shoved it through the new gap. Two men, already leaping through, smashed head-first into the makeshift weapon, instantly collapsing. Alicia reached down for one of their discarded weapons; Russo scooped up the other. Behind them, Crouch shoved the false street preacher backwards so that he fell over a table. Tourists scrambled aside as he fell, arms and legs pinwheeling. Through the ruined front door came a swarm of operatives, all carrying weapons with barrels aimed at the floor.

Alicia knew that wouldn't last.

"Down!" she yelled. "Get the fuck down!"

Most of the café's patrons were already scrambling to the floor. Those who couldn't or wouldn't, gawped. Alicia snatched a fleeting glimpse of a man calmly starting to raise his ceramic cup to his lips as the bullets started to fly. Crouch flung himself head-first, becoming tangled among a nest of tables.

Behind the bar, shelves crammed full of cups and saucers, flavored syrups and cafetiéres, all set against a mirrored background for effect, started to bounce and shatter and break. A gleaming, expensive-looking coffee machine fractured down the middle, perforated with bullets. Staff screamed, ducking fast.

Alicia was aware that the assault was happening on three sides, but still the hardest problem here was avoiding civilian casualties. As a third man stepped through the window to her left she put a bullet into his stomach, then grabbed him and spun him around. Bullets thwacked into his body without ceremony, answering her first question. Russo was down on one knee, aiming high, showering their attackers with chunks of falling ceiling. Alicia used the dead merc as body armor to glance around the corner of the devastated window. Outside, a narrow street was bordered by a small diameter railing with one of Venice's signature canals lying beyond, the gilded end of a gondola just passing beyond sight. There was a gap of roughly twelve feet to the sheer stone façade of the building on the other side of the canal.

No sign of mercs.

"Out!"

She crouched alongside Russo, signaling to Caitlyn to start crawling underneath the chair legs toward her. Every second that passed brought the mercs a little closer. A bullet shaved the edge of a table beside her. More barrels were starting to swing her way.

Alicia saw their moment of opportunity rapidly closing. She grabbed Caitlyn's outstretched wrist and pulled hard, employing all her strength to fling the girl toward the jagged gap. Caitlyn squealed but spun outside, jacket snagging on a glass spike.

Crouch heaved another table toward their assailants. It was all about distraction and escape now—they couldn't match firepower with firepower. A merc coming in from his left had already reached him. Crouch spun fast, ready to chop down at a gun hand but found himself faced by two whirling blades.

Alicia cringed. What the fuck?

One blade chopped into Crouch's jacket, drawing blood, the other simultaneously spinning across his neck, missing by a whisker. Crouch staggered, shocked and momentarily unfocused. The merc was a woman, of medium build and height and with short-cropped hair—a black stubble. Muscles bulged around her body armor.

Chick means business, Alicia thought and fired off a few rounds in her direction. The clip on her weapon was running low and needed saving.

Healey rolled into view from behind the bar, catching at Crouch's sleeve and dragging the man away from the female merc. Her cry of annoyance was more than primeval anger, it was a velociraptor at play. Alicia considered taking her out of the action, but before she could decide both Healey and Crouch were with them, pushing toward the window.

"Move!" Russo cried.

The mountain laid down some covering fire. Alicia stood at his side. Mercs dived every which way. The one who reached them met Alicia's front kick—a blow that broke ribs, yet still he forged on. Alicia smashed his face with the rifle's butt before kicking him over on to his back.

"Lay down and beg," she said. "There's a good boy."

Russo pushed her backward and she jumped over the lip of the window, into the narrow Venice street. Ahead of her tourists stared, most with backpacks or hand in hand with their partners. Another gondola plied the canal, with Caitlyn leaning over the metal railing toward it as if planning to flag it down.

"A fucking gondola?" Alicia shouted. "Are you mad? We could walk faster."

Healey dragged her away, flushing a little as if the idea had actually been his. Probably had. Alicia backed away from the devastated café fast, weapon raised as Crouch took point and led the retreat. Tourists jumped out of the way. The street was narrow enough to rub shoulders with most of them. Alicia and Russo shouted at them to lie down.

As if to prove their point mercs poured out of the café window, some shooting without caution even as they fell to the floor. Bullets hissed everywhere. A youth took a hit to the backpack, staggering but uninjured. Another screamed as bullets smashed into the wall beside his head. Alicia leapt over in an instant, took him by the scruff of the jacket, and hurled him shrieking over the railing and into the canal. Better there than dead. Russo dropped to one knee and returned fire. Crouch shouted that there was a bridge ahead, a way across the canal and off the deadly street.

Alicia took a glance. A bridge in Venice of course wasn't merely a bridge, it was an ornate arch spanning the greenish water, most of them imitating the Rialto Bridge of the Grand Canal. Alicia pushed people against the nearby walls as she backed toward it. The mercs followed in a group, and non-military part of Alicia's brain now caught up with the action. Who had orchestrated this? Kenzie? Riley? A brand new maniac?

Take your pick.

She reached the bridge with Russo a step behind and rushed across. Bullets pinged all around and cracked stone. Puffs of mortar dust floated through the air in front of her. They were fortunate the mercs were running and shooting at the same time, because if one of them suddenly grew a brain and stopped to take aim . . .

That made Alicia focus again on who might be following them. The abruptness of the attack surely ruled Kenzie out. The team hadn't come close to deciphering where the Hercules was yet, so why would the barmy bitch attack them so violently? Also, she had shown restraint back at the Hagia Sophia.

Then why did she go and kill poor old Naz?

The term "bug fuck crazy", came immediately to mind, but maybe that was just her. Terms from her army days constantly spun around her head. And there was another— "army" which some said stood for Ain't Really a Marine Yet.

Alicia shrugged it off as the bridge ended, its easy steps leading to yet another of Venice's tiny streets. Crouch picked up speed, shouting at people to get indoors. Buildings flashed by to both sides, most of them constructed of imposing stone. They entered a small square with a large parasol set in the center, tables and chairs all around. Other tiny streets led off in all directions.

"Only way to win is to lose them," Crouch said as loud as he dared. Alicia saw he was still bleeding at the wrist, the flow constant enough to leave a trail on the floor. They twisted down two streets, both mere alleyways with crumbling stonework to both sides. At the end stood yet another street full of shops, graffiti-covered walls, and a herringbone patterned pathway. Crouch set off at a sprint. Alicia glanced behind them and, over Russo's immense shoulders, saw their pursuers about twenty meters behind.

"Take one of 'em out," she said. "That'll slow 'em all."

"I'm bloody trying!"

Alicia swore. "Motherfucker, if you're not up for a shag and you can't shoot to save your life what the hell are you good for?" Quickly, she aimed and fired. A merc tumbled, crying out, and then screaming as his comrades tripped over him. Russo cursed her.

Ahead, Crouch suddenly switched directions, turning at an abrupt ninety degree angle. Alicia reached the crossroads just as Crouch, Caitlyn and Healey put their heads down and added speed, sprinting straight for . . .

What? Oh, no . . . shit!

"That's a canal! It's just a fu—"

Alicia clammed up as Crouch entered a particularly slender tunnel with the words Sotoportego Catullo, emblazoned across the top. Beyond, all she could see were the still waters. Then, in mid-sprint, Crouch jumped. Healey and Caitlyn were a step behind. Alicia ran in their wake, finally seeing their purpose.

A frigging gondola.

Trusting Crouch's judgement she readjusted her steps to make the leap as perfect as possible. The gondola was drifting along, even now tipping as Crouch, Caitlyn and Healey landed hard. The gondolier flipped over the side, too shocked even to utter a scream. Alicia jumped hard, seeing the end of the gondola already approaching, and landed inside the wooden vessel, aware that a meteor was about to strike.

Russo!

EIGHTEEN

Crouch struggled to his knees. Healey and Caitlyn were inextricably entwined. Alicia feared the worst and rolled over onto her back. Blue skies greeted her for less than second. After that the light was blocked out by something the size of a falling star. Her brain barely had time to register the coming impact before Russo crashed down, driving the breath from her body and sending the gondola up onto its side. Water flooded the boat, crashing over all of them as they struggled to stay inside.

The vessel righted itself, its sides shielding them from view, waves crashing from every side. The gondolier yelled in shock and anger, his hat floating away at his back, a sad counterpoint to his fury. Alicia couldn't even draw breath as she lay pinned beneath Russo, not for the first time in her life. Crouch grabbed hold of a red-covered seat, staring up the gondola's sharp curve to the prow-head. Wet brick walls, fungus and decaying facades lined the canal ahead, the lesser features of a gondola ride through the sinking city. The rowing oar was gone and the highly polished craft floated uneasily amidst its own waves, going nowhere. Crouch cast around, whispering for everyone to help.

Alicia gasped, still unable to breathe and pushing at Russo with weak arms. The soldier's face was an inch from her own, creased with surprise that he'd actually managed to land inside.

"Cool," he muttered.

Alicia flapped at him.

"What the hell's wrong, Myles? Are you trying to fly?"

With a deep, shuddering breath Alicia finally managed to get some air inside her body. Out of her peripheral vision she could see Crouch searching for a way forward and finding nothing. Very soon their pursuers would figure out where they had gone.

Russo knelt over her. Alicia gathered her strength and struck both hands against this chest.

"Move, ya fuckin' bouncing bomb!" Alicia had heard the word "fuck" was the most useful and often used word in the military vocabulary and always played her part in maintaining an average.

Russo rolled away, still struggling a little. Alicia tried to sit up, saw stars and lay back down. Crouch abruptly collapsed into the bottom of the craft.

"They're here," he murmured. "Hide."

Russo collapsed again without ceremony. Alicia groaned. "Bastard."

A moment passed, a few more seconds. The gondolier was still shouting from the water, attracting attention. Alicia knew that before long even the dumbest mercenary would shoot at the drifting wooden gondola.

"Grab your gun," she told Russo. "And be ready."

"Wait—" Caitlyn began.

"That'd be suicide." Alicia and Russo rose as one, instantly locking gazes with half-a-dozen mercenaries who stood at the tunnel's exit, scanning the canal. Before their enemies could open fire, Alicia and Russo sprayed them with bullets. Two fell into the water, two more collapsed back with wounds. Everyone began to yell.

"Gotta get away from here," Alicia said.

Crouch again scanned the area. "Don't they have speedboats? I was hoping for a speedboat."

"Banned them a few years ago," Caitlyn told him. "If you'd asked before you jumped . . ."

"I'll try to remember next time I'm in mid-flight. How's the ammo?" he called.

Alicia threw her gun at the water. "Out."

Russo waited and then fired a final burst. "Me too."

Crouch eyed the canal. "Hope there's a way out up ahead," he said and then leapt into the water. Taking his lead, Caitlyn slipped over the side just as Healey splashed beside her. Alicia stared at Russo.

"After you, Robster. The last time I went swimming the whole ocean exploded."

"Why am I not surprised?"

Russo launched himself over the side, creating a splash like a whale coming down. Alicia appraised their enemies' positioning before following suit. The female merc was leaning over as if she wanted to dive in and give chase, but someone was holding her back. Alicia knew that Crouch's reasoning had been sound—if the mercs dived in after them they would be vulnerable when the Gold Team climbed out. Their only advantage was to beat Crouch to the exit point.

Alicia hit the canal, trying not to swallow its dirty water and arrowing down like a fish, then jack-knifing forward. Soon, she was in front of Russo and then catching up to Crouch. "You know where you're going?"

Crouch flashed a grim smile. "Haven't the slightest clue."

"Fantastic." Alicia studied the way ahead. Sheer brick and stone walls reared to either side, festooned with green fungus just above the water line. Another bridge spanned the canal but there was no access to street level. Sirens sounded in the distance.

"Maybe that'll shake them off," Alicia said.

Crouch looked unconvinced. "I'm sure this is Riley's doing and believe me, nothing will ever shake him off."

Alicia curbed a sudden outburst, wondering why the hell Crouch had suddenly turned into the world's worst pessimist.

Truth was, she didn't know how many complex, random lines their boss was trying to thread together. Or why. Instead, she concentrated on swimming, the cold water beginning to bite at her senses. To her left both Healey and Caitlyn shot by, reminding Alicia of Flipper. Before she could say anything a gout of canal water entered her mouth, making her cough and splutter. Then, as she broke the surface again, trying not to imagine the germs she'd just ingested, she caught sight of what the two Flippers were aiming toward.

A wooden jetty dead ahead.

In fact a series of wooden jetties on both sides of the watery passage, where gondolas could dock to take on passengers. Alicia looked back, gauging their distance from the mercs. It would be close but they should have enough time to climb up and disappear. Did Riley know where they were headed next? She tried to remember the figures around them back at the café. Had anyone been listening?

Soldiers were good at spotting surveillance. But in a place like that one tourist just looked the same as another, innocent or not. And Caitlyn's revelation about Napoleon hadn't exactly been on the down-low . . .

Alicia watched as Healey reached the jetty first and began to climb the low wooden structure. The moment he reached the top he spun and held a hand out toward Caitlyn.

Alicia saw the merc appear out of the archway behind him, saw the gleeful smirk, the utter menace and opened her mouth to shout a warning. As she did so the merc threw a grenade in Healey's direction. The sound of its first bounce seized the soldier's attention.

"No!" Crouch cried out.

Healey's first instinct was to let go of Caitlyn, allowing her to fall back beneath the water. His second was to face the bouncing bomb alone, trying to gauge its terminus. Alicia could only watch, heart pounding, wondering why the hell he hadn't just jumped—

Healey leaped for the canal.

No time!

The grenade exploded in mid-air, fragments flying, its blast reaching Healey's airborne body, flinging it like a rag doll. The jetty itself shattered, timbers and spars bursting in all directions. Alicia dipped under the water for a moment, cursing herself for not having imagined that Riley would have the cunning to cover all exits. When timbers started landing on top of the water she waited a few seconds and then broke the surface again. Ahead, the jetty was collapsing, groaning to a watery extinction.

Healey!

She spotted the unmoving body a moment before it started to sink. With a kick and a sharp dive she shot down and forward, speeding toward Healey. Caitlyn, she could see, was already underneath the young soldier, trying to support his dead weight. From out of nowhere came another explosion, but this one deep, sonorous. The mercs were flinging grenades into the water. Alicia reached Healey, took hold of his jacket and hauled him above the surface.

Caitlyn grabbed his other side, her face a mask of anguish.

Crouch swam up. "Behind you!"

Alicia wasted no time trying to determine Healey's condition. Crouch pointed to a jetty on the opposite side of the canal. "If we're quick."

It was vulnerable, but their only means of getting Healey out of there quickly. Alicia immediately had an idea, handed Healey off to Crouch and grabbed hold of one of the jetty's timbers. Climbing fast, she glanced over to the ruined jetty.

Shit.

A merc was watching her, grenade in hand.

Crouch bobbed in the water below. "What the hell?"

"Climb!" Alicia shouted. "Just climb!"

Crouch urged Russo up first, shouldering Healey's weight until the big soldier gained ground. Healey was not moving, his limbs unresponsive, head hanging. Crouch heaved him up toward Russo's dangling arms.

Alicia gained the top of the jetty as the merc prepared to lob his grenade toward her. Crossing her fingers she cast around, hoping her outlandish plan would work. Seeing a meter long, thick plank of damaged wood at her feet she quickly scooped it up, whirled and eyed the suddenly airborne bomb.

Russo hauled Healey over the edge, eyes momentarily on her.

"Navratilova's got nothing on me," she said, swinging the plank and batting the grenade back in the mercenary's direction. It reached the middle of the canal before exploding in mid-air, shrapnel slamming into brick walls and shattering through windows.

Russo climbed up, dripping wet. "Nah, I'd say John McEnroe was more your role model."

Alicia eyed another grenade as it fell toward the jetty. "Hurry the fuck up, Russo. It won't be long before the bastards' brains catch up with their throwing arms and they time one to explode on impact."

Russo hefted Healey with a grunt. "Doubtful," he said, "from what we saw earlier."

Alicia batted another grenade away just as Crouch slithered over the edge, helping Caitlyn at the same time. The sudden explosion rocked the surrounding walls, echoing backwards and forwards inside the canal's narrow passage. Russo sprinted headlong toward their archway. Alicia hefted her wooden spar, trading jeers with their enemy.

"Is he . . . is he . . ." Caitlyn was spluttering, drenched and miserable and terrified. "Healey? Is he . . ."

Alicia's face turned grimmer than the pillars at the

entrance to Hell. "If he is someone's gonna wish they were never born."

<u>*NINETEEN*</u>

Crouch beckoned Alicia into the tunnel. "Hurry up! I've carried out my fair share of missions in Venice. I know just where to go."

Alicia ran, following the team onto Calle Frezzeria, still only a few street changes away from St. Mark's Square. Within minutes they were passing a vaporetto stop. Crouch slowed drastically for the water bus.

"Rio del Mancanton," he said. "Other side of the Grand Canal, and hurry!"

Money flashed, changed hands quickly. Russo didn't even try to explain Healey's situation, just laid the young soldier onto the bottom of the boat and hunched over him. Alicia analyzed their perimeter, as sure as she could be that they hadn't been spotted. How far did Riley's nasty little feelers reach?

Guess we'll find out soon enough.

Caitlyn was on her hands and knees beside Russo. "Zack! Can you hear me?"

Alicia dropped down. Healey's face was ashen and, oddly, even more boyish than usual. Alicia had heard reports of soldiers looking peaceful in death, fresher, but had never seen one until now.

"Oh, no."

Coming on the back of Komodo's shocking death this was almost enough to tip her over. Black spots started to fill her vision. Her breath shortened and a sense of rage began to take control.

Then Russo said, "He's alive."

Alicia felt a rush of hope. "Get down there, Caitlyn," she breathed. "Just snog that little bastard back to life if you have to. Whatever it takes."

Russo gently turned Healey's face away from the darkening skies. Alicia observed the tender gesture and fought down a surge of affection for the rough soldier. Now wasn't the time.

Their craft was cutting swiftly through the waters, closing in on its destination. Rio del Malcanton was situated in one of the seedier parts of Venice, not entirely safe during the nocturnal hours, but even that was not without its benefits. Crouch directed their gondolier where to dock and urged them all into the shadows as quickly as possible.

"It would be easier if all our phones and equipment hadn't just drowned," he said. "But I think I can still find my way around." After a moment he added, "Hopefully this place is still functioning."

Russo hefted Healey. Crouch led the way, threading through an ever-darkening series of streets before pausing outside a dilapidated bakery. Alicia could hear footfalls behind them, and smell the ever-present scent of decay in the air. The bakery stood at the top of a short flight of steps, its windows barred and its door strengthened with metal strapping. When Crouch knocked Alicia saw a face momentarily loom at the window. The footfalls at their backs had paused for now, but she sensed a presence, more than one, watching and waiting.

Not Riley's boys, she thought. They'd have nuked the place by now.

A voice enquired about their business. Crouch replied quietly, mentioning his name and what sounded like a password. Alicia suddenly knew where they were—one of the many MI5 safe houses around the world, most maintained with fully equipped dorms, cells, medical facilities, surveillance and interrogation rooms, and unmarked vehicles. A normal civilian would never be admitted, but a man like Crouch, with the password, and Caitlyn—ex MI5—might just pass muster.

The door opened. A head popped out. "Don't hang around then," the gruff Scottish tones rumbled. "They'll have your fecking bollocks off in ten seconds flat."

Alicia considered a reply, then decided better of it. Healey needed help not a smart-mouthed colleague. They followed the Scotsman into the bowels of the building, feeling for the first time in many days that they were surely free of observation.

"In here." The Scotsman opened a door and motioned toward a man wearing a white coat. "This here's Jack Hyde. We call him Jekyll. He'll take care of your man."

Later, over a microwaved plate of stew and several cans of John Smiths the group found time to relax. Crouch's password, it seemed, was good enough to allay any suspicions. The team were left to their own devices. Healey's initial exam and treatment would go on through the night so, unable to wind down enough to actually grab some sleep, they decided to ignore Riley and review their options. They settled roughly, sprawled around the tiny room with boots and gear on, drying out as best they could; the worry over Healey preventing any of them from trying to do anything normal. To a team member all they wanted to do was talk and be close to their fallen comrade.

"We are at an impasse," Crouch said. "We just can't prove that Napoleon took the Hercules at the same time he forcibly removed the Horses and transported them to Paris."

"Not an impasse," Caitlyn said through a mouthful of beef stew. "A standoff with known history. There's always something you can do about a standoff."

"For instance?"

Caitlyn indicated the laptop she had borrowed from the Scotsman. "Napoleon saved the French government from collapse by firing on Parisian mobs with cannons. He became General of the Army at twenty six. And he was beaten by Lord Nelson at the Battle of Trafalgar and the Duke of Wellington at the Battle of Waterloo."

"And this proves what?"

"He was a warlike figurehead, just like Dandolo, and no doubt a man of similar persuasions. He was an aficionado, a collector, a plunderer. He escaped exile in Elba and was, of course, married to Josephine."

"This proves nothing." Alicia, like Crouch, preferred to act as Devil's Advocate.

"All right, what about this? Napoleon ruled an estimated seventy million people and all of Europe, a level of political consolidation that had not been known since Roman days. I'm reading Constantine. Napoleon also produced medallions to commemorate his successes. Considered the most important by historians were the Five Battles Series, the first of which depicted Hercules holding a club and the Hydra's head."

Alicia flashed on the sculpture outside the basilica. "You're kidding."

"Nope. Some years after he stole the Horses one of Napoleon's favorite quotes was 'I have found the Pillars of Hercules!' Most thought he was referring to the new Paris. He once called Paris 'the new Rome of Napoleon.' And, most importantly, he displayed the Horses of St. Mark just as flamboyantly as did Dandolo, but clearly kept the Hercules to himself."

Crouch upended a beer. "He displayed the Horses? My history's a bit fuzzy there, I'm not sure I remember—"

"Only atop one of the most famous and important sculpted monuments in French history. The Arc de Triomphe du Carrousel."

"Of course." Crouch snapped his fingers.

"Depicting Peace riding on a triumphal chariot it is a derivative of the triumphal arches of Rome. In particular its inspiration is the Arch of Constantine. Is this enough coincidence and corroboration for you? If the Horses went to Paris it stands up that the Hercules went with them. Also, Napoleon became enamored of it and started comparing himself to Hercules in more ways than one."

"So Napoleon built an arch and had the stolen Horses placed on top, partly to rub it in the Venetian's noses," Alicia recapped. "A smaller version of the main Arc de Triomphe at Place d'Etoile yes?"

"Yes, originally it was intended as an entry way to the royal residence," Caitlyn read.

Crouch's head shot up, as if recalling something. "Now that's interesting," he said. "I couldn't quite put my finger on it just now, but what you said there—it rings an odd bell."

"Well, if you look at a picture of the Arc du Carrousel now you will see a very close copy of the four horses, each with one hoof raised as per Lysippos' original design and a replica of the quadriga itself. The French sure weren't shy in showing their admiration."

"And where was Napoleon at this time?" Crouch wondered.

Caitlyn tapped at the keyboard several times. "In 1828 he was dead, following a six-year incarceration at the hands of the British. I wonder if they knew how he cherished the Lysippos sculptures and tormented him about them. He was actually alive when the Horses were returned to Venice."

Crouch stretched and leaned back, tipping a beer. "I think it's worth a trip to France," he said finally. "What do you guys think?"

Russo shrugged. "No problem here."

Alicia sighed. "France just makes me think of one thing."

"Beauregard?" Caitlyn smiled.

"Close."

Crouch drummed the table top. "Hmm, perhaps we can use Reece Carrera again." He placed a call, waiting patiently for an answer.

"Yo, man!" Carrera's voice boomed over the loudspeaker. "The dogs of war are back! Was followin' your escapades in Niagara Falls, Michael. Good job, dude."

"How did you know that was us?" Crouch wanted to know. All personal details had been repressed.

"Well, 'cause I'm me. Eyes and ears like TNT. They explode over your antics, man."

"Good to know. Are you in Europe?"

Before Carrera could answer, Alicia grabbed the phone. "Hey, hey, do you know who this is?"

"Nah, just put Michael back on, sweetie."

"It's Alicia Myles."

"Alicia? I know Sophie. Sophie Myles. Never heard of you."

Alicia held the handset out to Crouch, an injured look on her face. "Guy's a knobhead."

Crouch mouthed "with a plane", then said, "Where are you right now?"

"London," Carrera said. "Filming."

"Ah, that's not going to work. Never mind. I'll be in touch, Reece."

"Cool. Oh, and tell Alice I said hi."

"Alicia!" Alicia shouted. "It's Alicia!"

Carrera chuckled. "I know." He ended the call.

Alicia's look of outrage transformed quickly to one of respect. "The bastard. He had me. Maybe not all movie stars are just muscles for show after all."

Crouch was already manually dialing a new number. Alicia zoned out for a while. This latest development—Riley—was a serious hindrance. Poor Healey was a casualty of circumstance but it could have been any one of them, and it could have been far worse. Every time she put a step forward, it seemed, life threw trouble her way. Kenzie was one problem, a combatant, but Riley was something else.

How many men did he control?

Alicia scanned her bedraggled crew. Crouch appeared quite neat, only his clumpy hair and the streaks of dirt on his face attesting to his recent escape. Russo sat hunched and solitary, a still dripping, lonesome and prickly heap of misery. Caitlyn perched in an easy chair, legs folded beneath her, worry etched deeply across her face, hair a spiky mess. This team was gelling nicely, still in its infancy but Alicia wondered how much further they could go together before a tragedy struck and forced it apart.

Crouch nodded at her. "I know a guy, ex SAS, whose business is near Venice. He'll fly us close to Paris."

"How close?" Alicia didn't like surprises.

"Well, he won't drop us off at the Eiffel Tower but we're not going to have to jump on a train either. Now, if you'll excuse me—"

Crouch rose and left the room, placing a call as he went. Alicia wondered who might warrant the private treatment. It was at that moment that the doctor stuck his head round the door.

"He's awake. And he's fine."

Alicia grinned, resisting the urge to leap up and bounce all over Russo. The man just looked too miserable and needed some serious cheering up. At least a major gust of relief helped to lighten his face and those massive shoulders lifted as a great weight detached. Caitlyn jumped to her feet and followed the doctor out of the room. Alicia lingered to wait for Russo.

"You okay?"

"Bloody hell, what do you think? You're a jinx, Myles. Whenever you're around the whole world goes to shit."

Alicia felt her heckles rise. "I wasn't around when you lost the Ninth Division. Maybe if I had been some people would still be alive."

The moment the words were out of her mouth Alicia regretted them. It wasn't fair to put that on Russo, or on anybody else. But Russo was playing with fire and needed to be reminded. The look on his face told her she'd gotten through the hard exterior.

"I'm trying to put that behind me," he said. "I thought we all were."

Alicia pushed past him, saying nothing, and walked into Healey's room. The young soldier was smiling as Caitlyn hugged him. Alicia grinned.

"You're looking better. "

"Feeling better."

"I bet. Well, get the hell off your arse then. Paris won't wait around for long."

"It's been there a while."

"Don't be a smartarse, kid. We're targets, and targets that move fast are harder to hit."

Russo grunted from behind. "Or easier to anticipate."

Crouch entered the room, almost certainly preventing a confrontation. The team leader seemed oblivious of the sudden tension.

"If you're able, Healey, we should move. The plane's waiting."

Healey swung his legs off the bed. "I don't need telling twice."

"Yeah, kid," Alicia said. "Stop messing about swimming in canals and trying to fly. We have a treasure hunt to complete."

Alicia hurried through the night, conscious of the space that surrounded the wide-open runway. It had taken them over an hour to reach this place and the entire team were anxious to be on their way. Not since she could remember had she actually felt so vulnerable. Riley had proved that he had the resources to strike anywhere, and however he wanted. *Is he out there now? Biding his time?*

Lining up a head shot?

The team moved fast, exiting a spacious almost empty hangar and heading for a grimy plane. Yes, she thought, it had seen better days, but then things were always better when they'd had a little "running in" time. Including people. Mostly people, actually. Humans were built to make mistakes, collapse and cry and then come right back up swinging. Life was nothing if it wasn't about taking chances. It was nothing if it wasn't about living. The only time it would pass her by was when she was lying in a grave.

And even then . . .

She followed Crouch, darkness her only ally. The gloom was so inscrutable it was like walking through a cave, apart from the slight breeze. The only light picked out the plane they were walking toward and all its flaws.

Kenzie's voice drifted from the murk. "Hands up and line up. I don't want to have to chop you people to pieces. Yet."

Alicia instinctively lowered her body, turning sideways to the threat, hands hovering over weapons that had been supplied back at the safe house.

Crouch looked ready to start stamping his foot. "How the hell did you find us again?"

Kenzie sounded smug. "I have my contacts too, Michael." She stressed the word "contacts" ever so slightly.

Crouch didn't respond, just looked worried. Alicia understood exactly what he was thinking. If his chain of international contacts was compromised . . . then he had no contacts at all. No trust. The world was falling down on Crouch as the enemies and victories of his past began to catch up with him.

"I followed you this far. Now, tell me the rest."

Alicia cleared her mind, practically willing her eyes to pick enemies out of the darkness. They were only ten feet from the plane and its lowered cargo door. Shelter in the form of old crates and even a rusted old car littered the disheveled airfield. The problem would be after they boarded the plane. Did Kenzie have enough firepower to take it down? Would she go that far? Alicia didn't know.

"You murdered Naz," she said. "You and me, we will have a reckoning for that one day."

"Go suck it, bitch. One day I'll stomp you into the ground."

Alicia's mouth almost fell open. She couldn't remember the last time she'd been spoken to that way. A lesson was in need of being taught. She said nothing, but the expression on her face could have frozen the polar north.

"So what do you want?" Crouch asked.

Alicia saw the pilots now approaching through the cargo hold, both looking uncertain. She knew from experience that any kind of tinder could set off a gun battle and almost spoke up to stop them, but what Kenzie said next stopped her dead.

"I want your treasure and then I want you all dead. In that order. Now talk before I change my mind and we move on to the next set of sad tomb raiders."

Kenzie was never going to let them go. The field was isolated, the perfect death trap. Alicia saw faces now as their enemy loomed unconsciously closer, itching for action. She saw eight, maybe ten faces and that of Kenzie's, tight with hate.

"There's no future here," she said, indicating their enemy. "We'd be doing the world a favor."

Crouch nodded almost imperceptibly. "I'm already there, Alicia."

Kenzie seemed to leap forward. "What are you saying?"

"That the treasure's still in St. Mark's Basilica," Russo

shouted unexpectedly. "With the Horses. They were never parted."

Alicia cringed.

"Then why are you about to hop onto a plane, Einstein?"

Russo caught flies.

Crouch stepped in. "Even if we knew, which we don't, we'd never tell you where the treasure is."

Kenzie nodded. "I know."

"Then what's next?"

"I guess you're making me do something I love. I'll have to torture it out of you."

Alicia spread her arms. "Go right ahead."

TWENTY

Alicia twisted away, knowing their enemy would already have weapons drawn. The rusted car stood at her back and she ducked behind the flat wheels. The noise she heard then, however, wasn't the expected gunfire, it was the roaring whine of a motorcycle engine. *No*, she thought as she lifted her head over the side. *Dirt bikes*.

Swerving left and right, men burst toward them. They must have wheeled them into position, she thought. That meant somebody had known the team's destination almost at the same time they did.

We're bugged. Or . . .

Not even the slightest hint of betrayal entered her mind. Not with this team. The approaching men all held compact machine pistols which Alicia recognized as the GEN4 Glock; deadly and accurate at the worst of times.

Her first shot hammered into a front tire, upsetting the bike's balance and sending its rider flying into the front of the immobile car. The crunch of impact told her they would no longer be a problem. By then, a second bike was scrambling up to her position, its muddy wheels spitting gravel like tiny missiles. Alicia ducked as she heard the clatter and bang of flying stones and a rush of dirt flew over the car and onto the top of her head.

"Bastard's gonna pay for that."

She rose, firing, but the merc had already leapt from his bike and crashed down upon her. Alicia felt the unexpected impact like a house collapsing and folded. Stars exploded before her eyes. The ground was a stunning, ungiving slab.

Her opponent tumbled past, his momentum unstoppable. Alicia groaned for an instant and remained immobile until some sense of reality returned.

It came in the form of Russo's boot being planted beside her head.

"No time for napping. We've a plane to catch."

Alicia struggled to her knees, head still spinning. The pilots had raced back to the plane's cockpit and started the engines. Power was already starting to thrum through the wings and down into the tarmac. Russo rendered the flying merc comatose as Alicia finally rose unsteadily to her feet.

"Wow, felt like I was hit by a truck."

"Let's hope it knocks some sense into you, eh?"

Alicia took in her surroundings in an instant. Kenzie was hoofing it toward the plane, Crouch and Caitlyn trying to cut her off. Healey stood before two dirt bike riders as bullets ripped up the road at his feet. Three more were slewing around the front of the rusted car.

Alicia and Russo picked up the fallen merc between them and hurled his body at the new arrivals. Their combined force was enough to take two down and make the third cartwheel over their wreckage. Russo finished them off fast as Alicia vaulted the front of the rusted car, still with a ringing in her ears, and returned fire at those who assailed Healey.

With a sudden lunge she was lucky enough to pluck one off his bike. The merc landed well though and was quickly up, confronting her. Alicia feinted, but fell to one knee, still unbalanced by her earlier collision. The merc struck at her. Quickly, she rolled on to her side firing upwards. The world spun again and a sense of nausea came over her. Healey backed up. A bike shot past, between them, a fire-breathing monster with intent to kill.

Crouch headed Kenzie off at the cargo door, planting his bulk before her advance. With a handgun steadied at his side he paused for a moment. "This isn't your game. Not anymore. Get out whilst you can."

"What? Go back to robbing Arabs of the petty treasures they've unearthed in the desert? To laying in the sand and dust for hours? To slogging through scorching sunshine and coughing my lungs up every night? I think not."

Crouch uttered a grunt of shock when Kenzie produced a gleaming weapon.

"A sword? Are you kidding?"

"It's a katana. Reforged from several swords originally made of true Damascus steel. My sweetheart."

Alicia staggered toward the confrontation. "Your sweetheart's a sword? And you melted down old Damascus steel to make it? Lady, you truly are a crackhead looney."

Kenzie swiped the sword through an arc as the plane's engines roared. The pilot's face could be seen through the open cockpit door and his voice drifted out.

"Get the fuck on! Now!"

Crouch dodged another swipe, pushing Caitlyn behind him. He raised his gun but in a flash Kenzie had smashed it out of his hand with the edge of the katana. Alicia saw him flinch and grab his arm in pain. Alicia found herself having to leap aside as the blade cleaved air where she had just been standing. The strike, as much as anything, confirmed Kenzie's willingness to do bloody murder . . . if it had landed it would have taken Alicia's face off.

As fast and deadly as a warhead, Kenzie barged both Alicia and Crouch out of the way and faced Caitlyn.

"Where the fuck's the treasure, bitch?"

The sword came down. Caitlyn threw herself to the side, landing hard on the plane's lowered cargo door. As Alicia whirled she saw that it was moving, slowly picking up speed.

Shit! This pilot's lifting off with or without us!

Russo and Healey struggled hard, first depriving the mercs

116

of their bikes and then battling them hand to hand. Alicia smashed a fist into Kenzie's back, then lifted her own weapon. Before she could fire Kenzie had flicked a knife in her direction. The first Alicia knew the blade was wobbling in her arm, barely piercing her flesh.

"You're faster than you look."

"And you're slower than I expected."

Alicia eyed the roaring plane, the cargo door already slowly closing. Crouch sprinted and caught hold at the same time as Caitlyn, pulling himself aboard. Alicia looked around for Healey and Russo.

"Get a bloody move on!"

Pivoting, she blew Kenzie a kiss and launched herself over the rising door, slamming her shoulder on rigid metal but refusing to release a yell of pain. She tumbled down the short slope, then caught hold of a strut and immediately scrambled back up to see if Healey or Russo needed help.

It was worse than she expected.

Healey lay on his back as a bearded merc kicked at his thighs. Russo struggled in the process of throwing another off and dealing with an approaching Kenzie. The sword flashed, floodlights glinting off the sheer blade. Russo rolled onto the merc, breaking the man's arm in the process. Healey was up on one knee, fending his attacker's brutal kicks to the side, skill and purpose helping him overcome his disadvantage. Alicia climbed up on to the edge of the rising tailgate, shouting, feeling the thrum of the engines picking up speed by the second, now at walking pace, now at jogging pace, accelerating.

"Slow it down!" Crouch told the pilot. "We have men out there!"

"Not a chance," the pilot called back. "I didn't get paid to fight Uma fucking Thurman."

Alicia made to jump over the tailgate but Crouch grabbed

her arm. "Wait."

The sound of a dirt bike caught her attention, then another as she looked up. Russo had climbed aboard one of the discarded bikes and hauled Healey up behind him. Kenzie was in hot pursuit on her own bike, holding the handlebars with one hand and wielding her sword with the other. Russo leaned over the front tire, obviously sensing every reason to tilt his body forward. Healey twisted around behind him, watching Kenzie's approach.

Russo gunned it, streaking toward the quickening plane. Alicia desperately sought a way to halt the ascending door. On the floor she found a thick wrench, probably used on this rust bucket for bolting the wings back on, and jammed it into the mechanism. There was a shriek of metal and a long groan, but the door did stop climbing.

Russo leaned hard over, swerving the bike as Kenzie drifted in close, swinging her sword at the same time. The blade sundered air that they had just occupied. Healey cried out, venting pent-up fear and frustration like a perforated exhaust. Kenzie sped up again, chasing the tail of the first bike, twirling her blade around her fingers like a cheerleader twirls her batons. Alicia saw a mad glint in the woman's eyes. In another second she had set her sights on the bike but knew even that was useless. The plane was bouncing and jolting, the bikes swerving and jarring. She'd be lucky to come within three meters of her enemy.

Russo cleverly veered right across Kenzie's bows, cutting her off and forcing her to brake hard. Kenzie came an inch from flying over the handlebars, but held on to her sword. Russo turned sharply again, opening the throttle now and racing hard for the plane. Screaming engines filled Alicia's ears. Tarmac flew beneath the wheels, rumbling past, a growling, unyielding river.

Crouch joined her at the top of the tailgate, gripping down

hard to hang on, their feet barely touching the floor of the plane. The wrench twisted slightly within the operating mechanism, causing the door to shudder. Alicia motioned frantically toward the approaching Russo.

"Come on! You're so close I can make out your wizened little eyes! Now push it!"

Russo couldn't have heard her, but he certainly understood. With a twist he opened the throttle to its fullest, forcing the bike to spring ahead. Kenzie followed suit half a second later, keeping pace. Alicia stared hard into Russo's eyes.

How the hell is he going to . . .

Russo said something to Healey. The young soldier reacted instantly and with complete trust. As Russo raced as close as he dared to the rattling tailgate Healey climbed his body, discarded his gun and crouched on the man's shoulders. Then, with an extra moment to steady himself he sprang from Russo's shoulders, crossing the space between the bike and the plane, hitting the top edge of the tailgate and sprawling over. Crouch clutched him by the arms, pulling hard, and Healey slid into the plane, taking Crouch tumbling with him.

Alicia stared at Russo. Already the plane was starting to out-accelerate the bike and would soon reach take-off speed. Russo was out of time.

Kenzie swung in from the right, sword flashing as she came in close. Russo deliberately braked so that she shot past, the sword clipping his front mudguard, and then juiced the bike for the last time.

All or nothing. Alicia saw the knowledge in his face.

The plane boomed, traveling faster by the second. The bike screamed at the edge of its capabilities. Kenzie wheeled around and attacked again, crazy for blood. This wasn't just about determining their destination, Alicia knew. Kenzie surely had the organization in place to be able to track a plane. The local council could track a bloody plane. This was about territory and one-upmanship and fear. It was a terrible challenge.

Russo stood up on the bike, balancing on tiptoes, then brought his feet up to the seat. The wheels hit a small ridge, making the whole skeleton bounce. Russo held on, hunched and with his teeth bared. The time came when the bike was as close as it was ever going to get. Alicia knew it. Russo knew it. The plane was starting to pull away.

"Slow down!" Alicia cried. "A few more seconds!"

"Can't," the pilot shouted back. "We're almost out of runway!"

Russo visibly gathered himself and then jumped. Alicia saw immediately that he wasn't going to make it. The runway was hard and brutal and landing on it at this speed would kill Russo immediately. Alicia flung most of her body over the top of the tailgate, balancing with the top of her hips, arms outstretched.

"Russo!"

A hand gripped hers, a disembodied, desperate hand. Russo clamped on, feet bouncing momentarily off the tarmac and drawing a bellow of pain from the large man. Alicia's other hand seized his other arm and pulled.

Dragging Russo was like dragging a full-grown walrus, and Alicia's body started to slip over the tailgate. Determined, she held on. She wouldn't let him go. Her eyes locked onto his and she could almost hear the conversation.

Let me go, Myles. Don't be an idiot.

Not a chance, asshole.

No point both of us dying.

Shut your stupid mouth.

Alicia slipped further. Russo's boots slammed against the tarmac again. The discarded bike bounced along with them for a moment, throwing sparks into the night before falling behind. Kenzie pulled up broadside, showing no emotion. The plane shrieked as it reached take-off speed and suddenly Alicia felt the angle change.

Fuck!

Only her powerful thighs were keeping her aboard now. Russo couldn't help; he had nothing to leverage with. It was a moment of utter madness, of one soldier keeping the other safe, of one friend refusing to let the other die. It was clinging on to hope until the very last thread had unraveled and the point of return was long gone.

The plane climbed. Alicia slipped over the tailgate with no thought for herself; only the need to keep Russo alive in her head. Strong crosswinds buffeted her, whipping at her face and hair. As the rushing tarmac beckoned strong hands suddenly grabbed her own legs, holding tight and trying to haul her back inside. But Alicia refused to give Russo up. The pulling hands weren't strong enough. A moment later a second pair grabbed hold, this time much further up, and also started to pull.

Alicia grunted in surprise and slid back inside the plane with her aching arms still attached to Russo's enormous hands. Both soldiers fell in a heap, exhausted and battered, too spent to acknowledge they were happy to be alive. Breathing and feeling pain were now the best sensations in the world.

At last, Alicia eyed Healey. "That's a hell of a way to cop a feel, Zacky."

Healey managed a tired smile. "Good job you've got some meat on your ass. Gave me something to grab hold of."

Alicia's eyes went wide. "Feeling brave aren't we? If I had an ounce of strength left you'd be over my bloody knee."

"Ooo, can't wait."

Crouch signaled for quiet. "So now we have Riley and Kenzie right on our tail. This is bad, folks. Not only are we in danger but everywhere we go ends up like a war zone. I'm really thinking we may need some help."

"Drakey?" Alicia said hopefully.

"No. The SPEAR team's busy chasing ghost ships." Crouch shook his head. "But this feels like war."

"It is war."

Crouch watched the tailgate finally slam into place, his eyes deep pools of unease. "Then let's start fighting back."

TWENTY ONE

Despite the mind-bending chaos, Crouch found himself drifting a little once the plane had reached altitude. Life as head of the Ninth Division had been peace and harmony compared to this madness. Perhaps it was the rigidity, the directness of military leadership, but since he'd returned to 'the field' nothing was written solely in stone. It was fluid, shocking, awash with decisions that were always second-guessed. It was living and thinking on your feet until your soles burned.

Ah, for the simple life.

Dreaming, thinking like a treasure hunter for all those years, hadn't prepared him for this. The world had changed since he'd been a boy. Black and white, and even grey, were dead ghosts from a misplaced youth. The heroes of his boyhood would never succeed in the world of today. Imagining an old Corgi toy, an ancient Hornby train set, just a poster stuck to the wall with its edges curling up, he wondered how they stacked up to the toys of 2015. Life moved on, but not just life. Technology surged but at the same time it seemed—morality shrank. Somebody, somewhere, was always getting away with pushing the boundaries. How much further could they be pushed?

Nostalgia pricked him. He studied his colleagues, thanking his lucky stars for those such as Alicia Myles and Rob Russo. They did understand today. They knew how the world had changed and what it meant to stay alive. They knew what it took to keep the world safe—even if the people they saved never knew or even cared. At the end of the day, they were the best at what they did and knew little else. Though they craved peace and love and normality, could they ever live with it?

Crouch reflected on his home back in London. He owned a flat in Hammersmith, just off the A4 that eventually led past Harrods and Hyde Park Corner. The flat was locked, silent now, a dark shrine to things that he thought he loved – Matchbox die-cast cars, fantasy books and magazines he'd found in the old Forbidden Planet store on Denmark Street, material unavailable in the UK—that kind of spine-tingling treasure hunt in old bookstores was lost forever now after the advent of the Internet. Some said it was easier, less frustrating; he thought it took away the magic of discovering hidden treasures. But wasn't that a boyhood thrill?

No. Even jaded adults like me love a gripping yarn. Once you pass a certain age your escapism comes through books or movies, not through real life.

He caught himself nodding, felt the crick in his neck, and came awake. The drone of the plane's engines was enough to soothe anyone. Even Alicia had her eyes closed—though Crouch suspected she might still be watching him. Alicia Myles had been the first woman accepted by the SAS and—apart from Mai Kitano perhaps—remained the most dangerous and capable woman he'd ever met. Her fire, her passion, came from seeking the next challenge, the continuing adventure. *What would happen if she ever stopped?*

Armageddon?

He shrugged unconsciously. There was only one man alive who could stop Alicia from self-imploding and that man was not here.

His thoughts turned to the dilemma at hand, and to the man who presented the greatest threat—Daniel Riley. Crouch had learned a valuable lesson the day Riley bought explosives and detonated a bomb in India. Never let your guard down. Of course, a valuable lesson sometimes had to be learned more than once but the fundamentals were there. After India, Crouch had become much more introverted, a quality that had later helped him become a leader. All that experience though, all those later encounters, never helped him understand what the hell had happened to Daniel Riley.

Life, he thought. *It was what happened to us all.*

And now . . . Kenzie. He shouldn't underestimate her as he once had Riley. She had already proved her willingness to do brutality, her lack of morality. She was down there with the parasites that fed off sewer scum as far as he was concerned. But two enemies? Two utterly ruthless, well-equipped and proficient enemies?

They needed help.

Crouch called a number and listened to the accent. "Hello?"

"It's me again. Did you figure out a way?"

"Oui. I can leave here for a few days. But no more."

"Good. I think we need you."

"And she? Does she need me?"

"We all do."

"Then that is good. Where she is involved I will always help."

"Oh, thanks for that," Crouch said a little drily.

"You are welcome, Michael. Where do you want me?"

Crouch moved to the furthest part of the plane and proceeded to convey everything he knew about Bridget McKenzie and the barest details about Daniel Riley. After a few minutes he paused.

"Is that it?"

"Yes. Now, are you sure the Pythians won't miss you?"

"I'm sure it can be done, mon ami. The downside is that I can only spare a few days. I will be in Paris when you are."

"Excellent. And you're not here to, um, make contact. Do you understand?"

Laughter emanated across the airwaves. "She will not even know I am there."

"Good. Perhaps we can find a few hours to debrief. It has been a while."

"We should. I have completed many undercover jobs for you before, Michael, but this . . . this one is the hardest."

Crouch was genuinely surprised. He had never heard Beauregard talk this way before. "In terms of?"

"In terms of craziness. I truly believe these rich fools want to blow up the world. Especially their leader. This Webb, if he can't get what he wants he will go nuclear. And he has the means."

"The Z-boxes?"

"Yes. And more."

"Okay, I'll find a way to pass the information on to Drake. We shall speak soon."

The line disconnected. Crouch watched Alicia and the others, pretty confident they hadn't heard any part of the conversation. Nevertheless, it had been imperative. Beauregard Alain was the world's master assassin. In theory, he could take Kenzie and her entire crew out in one night. The only problem with Beauregard was his penchant for powerful women—the Frenchman just couldn't help himself.

Crouch wondered if he should explain it all to Alicia. How Beauregard Alain had been a Ninth Division asset all along. How Crouch had recognized early the threat of the upcoming Pythian cabal and ordered him to go dark, to go rogue and get inside. Even Shelly Cohen—revealed later to be Coyote—had not known about Beauregard. Indeed it was she who had invited him to the Last Man Standing tournament and brought him to the attention of the Pythians. A masterstroke.

The rest was history.

Crouch sighed deeply and felt the stirring of an acidic stomach. Telling Alicia wouldn't be easy. He'd let her sleep.

Yeah, that would be best.

Let sleeping Amazonians, um . . . sleep.

TWENTY TWO

For Alicia, Paris lost much of its allure when she was forced to break into the Louvre. Nothing was ever the same after that, and she constantly wondered if her face remained on somebody's watch list. That said, if the hunt brought them here then the risk was immaterial. The chase would go on.

After landing they took a taxi into the city, found a café with rows of outside seating and commandeered three of the small round tables. It was late afternoon, the sun sinking but still warm. Droves of people wandered the streets, passing by in constant waves as if herded together by some unseen force. The smells of the city surrounded them, petrol and diesel mixed with strong coffee and garlic. Alicia took one look at the crowds and eyed Crouch.

"I know exactly what you're thinking and you're right," he said.

"Then what are we doing out here?"

Crouch paused as a waitress wearing a smart white shirt and black trousers squeezed by. "They know we're in Paris. The plane at least would have to file a flight plan. Who knows how many other methods both Riley and Kenzie might employ, but they're criminals at the top of their game. If they're not in the city yet they soon will be. We should quickly make a plan, and then go dark."

Alicia watched the waitress deliver a round of coffees. "Dark?"

"Split up," Crouch said easily. "It will make us harder to find, easier to hide. I suggest we meet again in two days."

Alicia took a moment to ponder, staring at the chalkboard

menu without really seeing it. Crouch had a point. The trail that led them here was reliable but also relatively thin. Crouch and Caitlyn would have some deep investigations to implement if they were going to uncover more clues. And besides, she'd had her fill of staring at old churches and monuments.

"Sounds good," she said. "I could do with some alone time."

Crouch nodded quickly. "We'll meet up in two days at the Arc du Carrousel. Midday. Don't be late."

Alicia finished her drink and walked away before Russo or Healey could suggest anything. The sun was sinking rapidly now, throwing shadows across the city, and though the last thing she wanted to do was wander the darkening romantic haunts they did at least offer anonymity. Her mind flashed on Claire Collins—the FBI agent she'd recently worked with who looked after the Disavowed guys—that girl worked hard and partied harder and, if caught in this city, would already be stoking up the dance floor. Alicia felt she might be approaching a turning point in her life, and needed time to compute and choose which of many options she might take.

Many options?

Sure, that was perhaps putting it a bit ambitiously. But her future did have opportunity, even if she couldn't quite see it yet. She took a narrow alley, enjoying the closeness of the walls and the phony darkness. Randomly, Laid Back Lex came to mind, she hadn't heard from him since Vegas. Her biker days had ended with the departure of Lex. She would never go back. Perhaps he had sensed that even then.

Unable to help herself she rang an old friend.

"Ay up."

"Drakey," she said softly. "How's it going?"

The Yorkshireman sighed softly. "Komodo's funeral was not easy. We miss you, Myles. Karin is taking it so hard."

"I'm sorry." This was not what she needed. "And the Sprite?"

"I dunno. Gone to Japan. I haven't heard from her."

"Do you really expect to?"

A sigh. "Nah. Not for a while."

"Did you catch another case?"

"Yeah. The Pythians are up to their new but old tricks."

"So," Alicia saw a way to liven the conversation up, "you're all missing me then?"

"Oh yeah. Every time someone doesn't take the piss it's like—where the hell's Alicia?"

"I like it."

"So why are you calling, Alicia?"

The question took her by surprise. She'd been trying to find her flow, her mojo, trying to turn a dark day and a dark outlook into a gossamer veil of silver. Drake's question brought it all back into focus.

"No reason. Just catching up." *And wondering who's willing to help me through the darkness that's coming.*

"I'll see you soon then."

"See you soon."

Alicia pocketed the phone, realizing now that she was staring along the River Seine and the city built around it. The rich golden glow of many lights filled the surrounding buildings, their deep radiance reflected in the waters that flowed below. The lighted balls of street lamps marched away as if marking the course she must take. Without waiting another moment she threaded her way back into the city and stopped at the first hotel she came across.

Using cash she paid for a room for two nights and made her way upstairs. Not used to and not happy about sleeping alone she crashed onto the bed and lay with her clothes on, studying the ceiling, listening to the noise of traffic and revelers outside, the bangs and clangs of the hotel and its returning guests, the sound of distant sirens.

Cities like this, they could never be still.

They possessed a soul that could never be quieted, a spirt that could never be quelled, an essence that demanded they move forward, and a heart that constantly craved for more.

As did she.

Crouch didn't comprehend the passage of time. After paying for a quiet room with high-speed Internet in one of Paris's classiest hotels he took advantage of the fact that the hotel staff clearly mistook the reason he wanted to whisk Caitlyn up to his room and made sure they would be granted privacy.

Once they were alone Caitlyn looked a little embarrassed. "Did you see the looks on their faces?"

"Sorry, no." Crouch was distracted as he powered on the laptop and arranged his notes.

"One of them even winked at me. Made me feel kinda filthy."

"Don't worry about it. In reality, I'm a major catch. A most eligible bachelor."

"That's not exactly what I was hoping to hear."

Crouch paused and laughed. "Yeah, sorry, I was a little side-tracked. The truth is—this couldn't be better. Now we're sealed off. We can work in peace, Caitlyn."

She appeared to shrug it off. "All right, all right. What have we got?"

Crouch took a moment to gather his thoughts. "Napoleon stole the Horses and the statue at the same time. Brought them both to Paris. Not long afterwards he erected the Arc de Triomphe Du Carrousel to better display the Horses. He compared himself to Hercules and Paris to Rome, though never directly. And there the Horses remained until defeat at the Battle of Waterloo sealed his fate. Following that, France ceded the Horses back to Venice."

"But not the statue?"

"We don't know that. If the trail leads back to Venice . . ."

Crouch allowed the sentence to hang, not liking where such a development would take them.

Brick wall? Dead end? A maze with no exit?

"We should read up on Napoleon and the Arc," Caitlyn decided. "And again, why is this statue so valuable to everyone? I never even heard of it."

Crouch threaded his fingers together. "Imagine this. The personal sculptor of the greatest known king who ever lived and the man who coached the creator of one of the seven ancient wonders of the world actually sculpted personal works by the hundreds. But none remain. Not one. The copies of his works are regarded themselves as ancient works of wonder. Now," he sat back, "imagine one work survived. Considered his greatest effort, it exists and is disclosed to and displayed only for the privileged and the ultra-wealthy. And even they cannot possess it. It is Lysippos' legacy."

"You truly believe works of art like this exist?"

Crouch barked out a laugh. "Don't show your naivety, Caitlyn. Of course they exist. Surely, over at MI5 you heard rumors of missing art. Freud's *Portrait of Francis Bacon*. Rembrandt's *Storm on the Sea of Galilee*. Picassos. Caravaggios. Even a Raphael that disappeared in 1945, taken by the Gestapo to decorate Hitler's Berlin residence. It has not been seen since except in an episode of the Simpsons."

Caitlyn blinked rapidly. "I'm sorry?"

"Yeah, go figure. More conspiracy theory for you. And they're merely a snip of what's out there. Do not tell me that wealthy individuals and secret groups all around the world aren't acquainted with that's going on."

"Private showings?"

"At the very least."

Caitlyn poured herself a glass of red wine. "Well, Napoleon conquered much of Europe through the Napoleonic Wars—a chain of key conflicts fought on an unprecedented scale. He fought sixty battles, only losing seven, most of which were at the end of his career. The most famous defeat—at least for us—is at the Battle of Waterloo. After Wellington's victory the allies then reversed all French gains at the Congress of Vienna."

"All French gains?" Crouch picked up on the statement. "Is that when the Horses of St. Mark were ceded back to Vienna?"

"Yes. The end of the wars resulted in the dissolution of the Holy Roman Empire and," she paused, "Britain became the world's foremost power for the next century."

Crouch narrowed his eyes. "Really?"

Caitlyn nodded. "The Duke of Wellington was a conquering hero as Napoleon had been before him."

"And Waterloo? Anything there?"

Caitlyn took some time to read through a wealth of information, finishing half the bottle of red wine and starting to feel decidedly tipsy. "Fought on Sunday 18 June 1815. Wellington called the battle 'the nearest-run thing you ever saw in your life'."

Crouch listened for a while, perusing information on the Arc du Carrousel as he listened. When Caitlyn took a breath he interrupted. "I believe the Arc is more important. Known as a triumphal arch our Horses were placed atop it. Finished many years before the more famous Arc de Triomphe it was a monument to and a focal point for Napoleon's victories. It inspired the design and construction of London's Marble Arch. Every one of its bas-reliefs depict Napoleon's victory in battle."

"None of that brings us any closer to the Hercules."

"No," Crouch mused. "No it doesn't."

At that moment there was a knock on the door, a soft rap. Caitlyn jumped, eyes wide, but Crouch appeared unnerved.

"Don't worry."

"You're expecting someone?"

"Yes. I'm just surprised he didn't enter through the window."

Crouch rose and unlocked the door, welcoming the figure dressed all in black. When Beauregard shrugged off his knee-length woolen coat Crouch saw that he was attired, as usual, in the skin-hugging jumpsuit.

"Oh crikey, man. Does it have to be so tight?"

Beauregard slipped around him, a sinuous shadow. "We have little time."

Crouch turned in time to see Caitlyn staring at the newcomer, a new blush creeping up her exposed neck to her face. "Oh dear."

"I'll say," Crouch said. "Sit down."

"I prefer to stand."

Caitlyn grinned. Crouch shook his head. "Whatever. This is all the information I have on both Kenzie and Riley." He handed Beauregard a sheaf of papers. "I think Argento at Interpol will be able to help with Kenzie's travel plans, though Riley might not be so easy. He's always been a slippery one. Call me when you have information."

"Consider it done."

"Good. And Beauregard?"

"Yes." The well-built man half-turned toward his boss.

"No sneaking around Alicia, do you understand? You two don't have the time or, more importantly, the necessity to be getting to know each other."

"I think they know each other pretty well." Caitlyn tried not to stare and gulped even more wine. "At least from what Alicia described to me."

Beauregard turned his swarthy face upon her. "And what did she describe?"

"Ah, well, ummm . . . ."

Crouch came to her rescue. "Please just get the information, Beau. The entire team is up against it here."

"I will do my best." The Frenchman whirled, swept up his coat, and exited the room. Crouch locked the door in his wake.

"I guess mum's the word," Caitlyn said. "Which is a shame since I've never seen such perfect buttocks."

Crouch shuddered. "Rein it in dear. You're beginning to sound like a certain Miss Myles who must never know Alain was here."

Caitlyn coughed. "Yes, I'm sure I've had too much to drink. Sorry, sir."

Crouch shrugged. "Well, it is Paris."

Caitlyn swilled the remains of her wine around the bottom of her glass. "His appearance does raise one or two questions though, sir. Nobody's ever been sure which side he's on."

"He's on my side," Crouch told her. "And that's all for now. I intend to explain myself soon but now is not the time."

Caitlyn nodded. "Fine. Agreed."

Crouch settled back down. As his eyes skimmed the screen a thought occurred to him. "You mentioned a Congress of Vienna, where all of France's gains were returned."

"Yes."

"Well, a congress is a meeting, right? A great, important meeting between heads of state, perhaps. And with meetings like that there is often paperwork."

"Every time, I'm thinking."

"So if we could get a look at the official document that relates to the Congress of Vienna then we would see what various lands, arts and others works were returned to their owners."

"Yes, the Horses were mentioned briefly."

"On the Internet." Crouch said. "What about the original document?"

"You're thinking it may have been altered for the Web?"

Crouch raised a brow. "Haven't most official and governmental things? An omission here and there keeps the world oblivious."

"The original . . ." Caitlyn deliberated. "Ah, it's in the Louvre."

"Excellent. Is it on show?"

"To a degree. They won't just let you take it down and have a flick through."

Crouch smiled for the first time. "We'll see about that, won't we? My own assets may not be on the outside, Miss Nash, but they're just as large as our French friend's."

This time, Caitlyn choked on her wine.

TWENTY THREE

The next morning their first act was to visit the Arc de Triomphe du Carrousel. Crouch led Caitlyn to the Place du Carrousel and the two stood in the early chill, staring up at the grand monument.

"Still feeling ropey?" Crouch asked, giving her space.

Caitlyn groaned. "The next time I decide to swig an entire bottle of red wine please just kill me first."

"I'll do better than that," Crouch said. "I'll render you unconscious. That way you get to see tomorrow."

"Sounds fantastic."

Crouch made a move toward the arch. "Built between 1806 and 1808. A high central arch flanked by two smaller ones." He motioned. "See all the bas-reliefs?"

Caitlyn made an agreeable sound, taking in the raised sculptures across the front of the arch. She moved aside as an older man knelt beside her to take pictures. Crouch waited until he wandered off.

"The quadriga on top is what we're really interested in. It is a direct copy of the Horses of St. Mark but even so, while the French had them, the originals were still brought up for special occasions."

Caitlyn seemed to fathom his meaning despite her stupor. "So the originals were usually hidden away?" Her face broke into a grin. "Shit, that's perfect. The masses get to marvel at a copy whilst Napoleon and his cronies ogle the original."

"You got it. And that poses the question—what else did they ogle?"

Caitlyn nodded, saying nothing.

Crouch continued. "It's likely that, like most of these triumphal arches, there are rooms inside or perhaps an underground chamber. Who knows what goes on beneath our feet?"

"Tunnels?" Caitlyn questioned. "Secret passages and byways?"

"Perhaps. Every old city, especially those with an underground train system, has them."

"All right." Caitlyn looked around. "Now we just need to prove it."

"It always comes back to the Horses," Crouch said. "Until now. It says here that they were looted and then paraded in front of Parisians along with a vast war booty in much the same way that Roman Emperors commemorated their victories."

Caitlyn took several deep gulps of water. "Which leads us to the 1815 Congress of Vienna."

"And to the Louvre," Crouch said. "Which I believe is over there."

The most visited museum in the world welcomed the new arrivals as it did almost everyone else, first through the large glass and metal pyramid and then a descent into a spacious lobby whereupon they would be required to re-ascend into the main buildings. Though the hour was still early the area was jam-packed. The ambiance was pleasant, excitement helping to stimulate tired tourists in their quest for ancient wonders. Crouch paid whilst Caitlyn used the old-fashioned method to locate the document that related to the 1815 Congress of Vienna.

"Here," she waved the guide book at him when he returned. "Richelieu Wing. There's some kind of temporary exhibition hall where it's being housed for now."

"Good. We have thirty minutes to get there."

"We do? Why?"

"I'm sure you remember me mentioning my assets?"

Caitlyn colored a little. "It was a rather memorable moment."

"A curator will be meeting us there and, hopefully, allowing us a few minutes access to the document."

"Is that long enough? How big is it?"

"Oh, it's big but the curator knows his stuff. He should be able to help."

Caitlyn allowed Crouch to lead the way, trying to imagine how wonderful it must be to at least know someone who knew someone who could make things happen. Of course, Crouch had been in authority for decades and had traveled the world dozens of times. If a person was clever he never missed an opportunity to make a valuable contact. Crouch, to his team's unceasing gratefulness, appeared to have taken that advice wholly to heart.

The Richelieu Wing stretched before them, lined to either side by old masterworks, a perfect white vault above, allowing a huge amount of inspirational light to shine down upon the ambling worshippers.

As they strolled arm in arm to help deter onlookers Crouch spoke softly. "As things stand, I don't like introducing outsiders. We don't know where Riley has bribes and hooks in place. But with this I had no choice. Without this curator's help we're all hammers striking at a nail made of rubber. Getting nowhere fast."

Caitlyn squeezed his hand. "Riley's sent you all off kilter, huh? I've never seen you like this."

Crouch gave a half chortle. "Caitlyn, despite the hand-holding, we've known each other for about five minutes. You don't know me and I don't know you. Not really. It's a credit to you that I already regard you as an indispensable member of our team."

"Well, thank you. My time at MI5 was vital. In one way I'm sorry it was cut short, but in another . . ." she indicated their position. "I never would have come this far."

Crouch asked a question that had worried him since he first heard about Caitlyn Nash and her burnout. "Did MI5 fail you?"

Caitlyn instinctively pulled away, but then came back to show her reaction had been unintentional. "No. They were entirely professional. I guess you could say it was my father who failed me."

Crouch did not want to pry any further. "I'm sorry."

"Don't be. It wasn't your fault, nor mine. To save myself from what happened I would have to turn back time."

Crouch gave her hand a lighthearted squeeze. "Oh, the wrongs I could right . . ."

Caitlyn pointed toward a floor sign, showing the way to the temporary exhibition. "We're here."

Crouch stopped before a fourteenth century French painting, pretending to have an interest but in reality scanning their peripherals. The Richelieu Wing in his experience had always been the quietest, probably because it didn't contain any of the more famous works of art popular in the Denon Wing, but it still maintained a high frequency of foot traffic. After a minute with no warning sensors triggering in his brain he moved along.

A narrow offshoot to the Richelieu Wing appeared ahead. On one side stood a row of all-glass display cabinets, stretching from floor to ceiling, with knee-height pedestals inside upon which sat many documents and manuscripts. Black signage ran along a supposed centerline. Crouch quickly moved to the one that read 'Congress of Venice 1815'.

Caitlyn almost touched the glass in her urgency, but Crouch pulled her away. "We're ten minutes early."

Caitlyn whistled. "I can't believe we're about to read

passages from one of the most important international conferences in European history. It's . . . a little sublime."

The official document before them, under glass, was yellowed but perfectly legible. The title page read: Acte du Congrès de Vienne, Du 9 Juin, 1815. It was signed, though Crouch could not make out the name, and attested as the 'official edition'. *Of course*, he thought. *Otherwise why would it be displayed in the Louvre?*

A man approached noisily, dressed in a blue suit and sporting a bright red tie. His hair, professionally styled, swept up over the top of his head into a fin-like shape. He was much younger than Crouch had expected.

"Are you Amaury?"

"I am. We should be quick." Amaury's eyes darted left and right as if expecting a surprise attack at any moment.

Crouch nodded. "My thoughts too. You seem nervous?"

"It is not often one of the museum's directors wakes you in the middle of the night, rips a man out of his bed and orders him to allow a person he doesn't know a private, uninterrupted viewing."

"It isn't? I would have thought it happened more often than most people would imagine."

Amaury almost smiled. "I can't speak for that."

"Of course. Carry on."

The curator produced a small key, inserted it into an inconspicuous silver lock, and slid a portion of the glass aside. The gap was enough to allow only Crouch access. Caitlyn hovered at his shoulder.

"Please," Amaury insisted, holding an object out. "Use these and have care. No fingers. Flex the pages as little as possible. Do not touch them with items of your clothing."

Crouch knew the guidelines well. His love of archaeological history had sent him down every avenue in the past, and that included how to handle ancient manuscripts or parchment.

The trouble was, the ink was no longer firmly attached to the pages. Forcing anything was out of the question. Amaury was holding out a pair of book snakes, lead weights inside fabric tubes used for holding a book open, essential for handling the document.

"Don't worry. I will be careful."

"Hmm. I reserve the right to worry."

Crouch handled the document, conscious of Amaury's every tiny intake when he suspected Crouch may have the snakes one or two millimeters off. The curator listened to Caitlyn's contrived spiel regarding the so-called Horses of St. Mark and thankfully knew immediately what they were looking for.

"I understand. It is a passage that clearly indicated the return of the Horses to Venice and yet also alludes to the unknown. I'm surprised you have heard of it. The passage is totally anonymous."

Crouch stopped himself from laughing aloud. "You mean you don't get many visitors asking about the Congress of Vienna these days?"

Amaury shrugged. "Most are not so rude. With this treaty they redrew Europe's political map, enforced Napoleon's abdication and restored lands to many that France had plundered. Though not always their treasures," he admitted at the end.

Crouch waited for the curator to step forward, take over the snakes and find the passage. He had no idea what he was looking for, but Amaury's words gave him a shard of hope. Minutes passed. Crouch eyed their surroundings, in particular their only way out, and motioned that Caitlyn do the same. Their newest recruit wasn't a soldier and didn't possess a soldier's instinct, but she was always willing to learn as best she could. Another minute ticked by. The sound filtering from the Richelieu Wing grew steadily louder as the day wore on.

As Amaury flicked past the pages Crouch saw much white parchment covered in spider-web writing, some adorned by thick red, waxen seals.

Amaury grunted. "It is here. This is your passage."

Crouch thanked him and waited for him to move aside before bending toward the page. Written on surprisingly white paper in tiny lettering were several passages. Crouch took his time to read them all.

"All right." He smiled. "I have the official part where the Congress ceded the Horses back to Vienna. All good and proper. It makes no mention . . ." he tailed off.

"Makes no mention?" Amaury enquired.

"Wait." Crouch was surprised to find that, amongst all the bureaucratic, legal language there sat a small, inconspicuous passage that almost went unnoticed. The only reason he didn't skim it over was that it was written in a different style to everything that came before.

"Is this the passage you referred to?" he asked Amaury, pointing but careful to stay away from the page.

"Yes, that is the one."

Crouch turned to Caitlyn, unable to hide the smile. "I think we've found a bloody fine clue."

TWENTY FOUR

Crouch read the passage aloud:

"From an Ancient Wonder's home to the Domus,
"From the Golden palace to the Emperor's Circus,
"The First riding above all,
"The Second supporting the wall.

"From the Floating City to the New Rome,
"Undivided as Lysippos intended,
"The Tarentum—the strength, the bolster,
"The Quadriga—the show, the vision.

"Then sundered materially as never in spirit,
"One always the show,
"The other below,
"By the Pillars of Hercules he endures,
"A part of the soil,
"Hiding among New Arches envisioned,
"To the victor the spoils."

Caitlyn peeked over his shoulder as he recited the passage. Amaury shifted from foot to foot, still clearly nervous. Both of them looked at Crouch at the same time.

"Well?" Caitlyn asked. "Do you know what it means?"

"I haven't a bloody clue," Crouch said. "But let me copy it down. I take it you have no objection to me taking a picture?" He glanced toward the curator.

"It is the Louvre," the Frenchman said in assent. "It is what is expected."

Crouch snapped several photos and then thanked the

curator. After the man locked up and walked away Crouch allowed himself to break into a wide grin.

"This is why we do this," he said. "For breakthroughs like this. For the discovery of lifetimes. For the thrill of the chase. This is what it means to be a treasure hunter."

Caitlyn threw her arms around his neck before she could stop herself, exuberant as ever. Crouch immediately coughed and grunted and regained most of his English reserve.

"Um, okay. Well, let's go then. Figure this out tonight and then round up the gang."

"You make them sound like the Scoobies."

"Are you kidding? I'd kill for the Scoobies at a time like this."

Caitlyn nodded. "Wouldn't we all."

"Now how the hell do we get out of this place?"

"We go against the flow, Michael. Isn't that what we always do?"

TWENTY FIVE

As the day passed, Alicia found solitude increasingly demanding. Another walk along the Seine, another coffee in a café, one more hour behind a desk trying to chart the future course of her life. One more sheet of blank paper. A distant study of "normal" people, and of how they went about their daily lives. It all seemed so alien to her. It had been said time and time again that career soldiers could never adapt to a regular life. Looking at typical habits and routines, Alicia could easily understand why.

The first man who beat her to the last bottle of milk on the shelf would end up crushed at her feet. The pushy woman who barged past her in the street would find her head in a handbag, still attached of course. The idiot wandering along in the flow of human traffic, obliviously texting or flicking at his cell screen as he walked, would run right into the point of her elbow.

As her thoughts turned darker, Alicia knew it was time to seek some company. First she rang Russo and thought, *What the hell, why not make it a threesome?*

Russo and Healey turned up together. Alicia suspected they'd met some time earlier, but said nothing. Russo sat down on the bench beside her and stared at the huge Egyptian obelisk at the center of the Place de la Concorde.

"They all seem so . . . unaware," he said, referring to the people. "Carefree."

"They're not," Alicia said. "But for today, and because of people like us, they can be."

"Do you think we'll ever get to do that?" Russo said.

Alicia stared at him, surprised how close he was to her way of thinking. Silently, she shook her head. Healey voiced an objective of one day becoming a model civilian but Russo pointed out the fact that he was barely out of pre-school.

The hours passed. The day wore on. The soldiers took stock of their surroundings and ensured all was safe. It was what they did. Sentinels watching over the living, as those who had gone before watched over them. Uncles, brothers, fathers, mothers, sons and daughters forever lost but never forgotten.

Memory preserves them all.

Darkness fell for the second night and Alicia was looking forward to an early start the next morning. Crouch had texted to explain what they had found, but demonstrated no headway yet. She said her goodbyes to Russo last after forcing Healey away an hour earlier and topping her quota of the expected "time you were in bed" wisecracks, then took a steady walk back to her hotel. Even before she entered the room she knew it was occupied.

Call it sixth sense, SAS training, perception by a woman at the top of her game. Call it luck. She knew. And when the door opened inwards and the figure loomed she was ready.

Lightning quick, she jabbed to the throat, poked at the eyes, kicked at the knees. The figure danced back, staggering as the lower blow struck home. Alicia followed it up with another blitz attack, slamming her knee in hard—once, twice, three times—but each blow was blocked by a raised elbow. No words were passed.

The figure rolled away, a jacket left in its wake. Alicia bounded forward, felt brief contact with the bridge of her nose, and stopped, tears blinding her eyes. The next blow struck her sternum, causing her to gasp, ripping her T-shirt. She retaliated in a second, fast blows to the body, digging her fingers into the figure's own clothing and ripping a good chunk of it away. Hard, hairless muscles were revealed. The man attacked in a blur, all darkness and distorted silhouette, spinning around her body in a full circle and ripping the rest of her T-shirt away. Alicia didn't let up; there was no modesty in this kind of battle.

A feint to the groin and a punch up into a falling chin made her opponent see stars. She stepped in and tore the man's black clothing down from the chest to the waist. He recovered fast, dropping to one hand and kicking with both feet. The strikes took Alicia by surprise, made her fall flat on her ass. Before she could move, both her shoes were ripped from her feet. Alicia couldn't help but mutter in surprise.

How the hell . . ?

But he wouldn't get the better of her, she was determined. She knew where certain vulnerabilities lay. As the man ducked in again she rose powerfully and then dropped quickly to her knees, shredding the rest of the material that covered his body.

The man paused in shock.

"Be careful, Beau," she breathed. "If I manage to get hold of that thing I'm gonna use it to twirl you above my head like a whirlycopter."

The man kicked at her shoulder. Alicia forced herself to concentrate but found it hard to avert her eyes. "Oh wow, I've so missed—"

In a move too fast for her to comprehend, Beauregard spun her around so that her back was pressed into his body and then launched her onto the hotel room's bed. Two seconds later he'd ripped her trousers off. Alicia, panting, lay still, then slowly turned her head to look coyly over her golden shoulder.

"So? You waiting for an invite or are you gonna pound that?"

Beauregard needed no second request. Falling atop her he put his lips close to her ear. "Are you ready for me?"

"Fighting my boyfriend always turns me on."

"That is what I thought."

Alicia propped a cushion under her hips. "For fuck's sake, be careful."

"Ah, if only I had a franc for every girl who asked me that."

"Fuck you."

"No." Beauregard pressed into her hips. "I think you have that backward."

Later, bruised and spent, Alicia rolled over to create some space between herself and the Frenchman. What had promised to be a spectacularly boring evening had turned into something far more satisfying, but there were still questions to be asked.

"Beau? What the bloody hell are you doing here?"

"Isn't that obvious?" The master assassin thrust his hips at her.

"Quit that. I'm serious. Who are you working for, Beau. And why are you in Paris?"

Beauregard pulled the sheet across his body, giving Alicia a moment's regret. He plumped the pillows behind his head and sat up. "Look, Alicia, I cannot answer your questions yet."

"Yet?"

"Yes. The time is soon, but it is not my decision."

"Shit Beau, you had better be working for the good guys. If you turn out to be working for those asshole Pythians I'm really gonna have to kill ya."

"Your patience will be worth it."

"Now you sound like one of those business answering machines." She switched to a tinny accent. "We appreciate your call. It is important to us. You are fifth in the queue. We are currently servicing Trevor. Please bend over and let us take you—"

"Look." Beauregard interrupted her and leaned forward. "I have never been this far on the inside, undercover. Every moment I remain with you my life is in danger, but I did remain."

"In danger?" Alicia repeated. "Is that why you finished so quickly?"

Beauregard turned away, frustration flashing across his features. Alicia relented and reached out to him. "So tell me this then. What are the Pythians up to now?"

"Nothing but their usual megalomaniacal bullshit. Tyler Webb's incessant needs center around ghost ships and Saint Germain. I fear if he does not get what he wants then he will turn our world to ashes. And his needs—they're demonic to put it mildly."

"Demonic?"

"Subjugation. Domination. Societies in chains. Death squads. I could go on."

"Please don't."

"And if he becomes frustrated . . ." Beauregard let it hang.

"So you're the inside man. And you won't tell me who you work for. All right. I can live with that but only for a short while, Beau. You get me?"

Beau nodded, his powerful body shifting slightly beneath the sheets and drawing Alicia's attention. "Already, the Pythians are recruiting new primary members. I have only two names so far—Julian Marsh and Zoe Sheers. But it is a start. The names have been . . . passed on."

Alicia sensed that her lover wished to tell her more. Wanted to. Her intuition was rarely wrong and she truly believed Beauregard was genuine. Despite the fact that whenever they met she always seemed to end up with a set of fresh bruises.

"And now to a more serious issue," she said, leaning forward. "Never, ever, try to cover yourself up when we're alone again. I like you naked."

Beauregard gave an exaggerated sigh. "Of course."

Alicia hesitated. "And just so we're clear this time. You wanna fight first or fuck?"

"It is up to you."

Alicia laughed. "Oh, I know that, Beau. I really do."

She climbed on top.

TWENTY SIX

In the shadow of the great Arc de Triomphe the Gold Team regrouped. Though surrounded by light, noise and groups of locals and tourists they felt as unobtrusive a crew in Paris as they were ever likely to get. Alicia knew none of them had had time to process the Riley or even the Kenzie angle yet. A team like theirs simply couldn't disappear off the grid forever.

Action would have to be taken.

"It's a clue buried deep within the Congress of Vienna." Crouch pitched his voice below the timbre of the crowd. "But on the same page that ceded the Horses back to Venice. Listen up and tell me what you make of this:

'From an Ancient Wonder's home to the Domus,
'From the Golden palace to the Emperor's Circus,
'The First riding above all,
'The Second supporting the wall.

'From the Floating City to the New Rome,
'Undivided as Lysippos intended,
'The Tarentum—the strength, the bolster,
'The Quadriga—the show, the vision.

'Then sundered materially as never in spirit,
'One always the show,
'The other below,
'By the Pillars of Hercules he endures,
'A part of the soil,
'Hiding among New Arches envisioned,
'To the victor the spoils.' "

Crouch finished and looked expectantly at the others. Russo grunted. Healey stared. Alicia put their expression into more eloquent words.

"Fucked if I know."

"Well, luckily for you guys Caitlyn and I have been working on it all night," he said. "We have some of the stanzas figured out. It's a history, a chronology if you like, of the Hercules Tarentum and the quadriga. 'From an Ancient Wonder's home' is . . ." he paused.

Alicia shrugged. "There were only seven. And I'm guessing this also revolves around their maker so I'm guessing Alexandria."

"Yes. The Lighthouse of Alexandria was one of the seven ancient wonders and where Lysippos created both pieces. Now, through some web research we have determined that the Horses then came to Rome. The Romans certainly knew of Lysippos through the writings of Pliny—there was a huge market for his work. A big emperor needed a big Lysippos to prove his power, his manhood. So, according to the records the Horses made their way to Emperor Nero who displayed them in his Domus Aurea, which was a huge landscaped villa built at the heart of ancient Rome around AD 68. Pliny the Elder was there whilst it was being built, this so-called Golden House, and mentions it in his writings."

"Is it also the Golden Palace?" Alicia asked.

"Yes, nicely thought out. The next two lines are a reference or a clue to the actual pieces, of course, possibly a way of covertly alluding that the Hercules goes in tandem with the quadriga. Suggestions of spectacle and strength—the Horses and the Hercules. It also hints that the Horses are for display whilst the Hercules is concealed, a suggestion that is reinforced later in the verses."

Caitlyn broke in as Crouch took a breath, unable to curb her enthusiasm. "Right! Next verse. 'From the Floating City to the New Rome'. It's now you realize that they skipped Constantinople, see? Where we know the Horses stood atop the Hippodrome. We think this is because the people who wrote these verses in 1815 and ceded the quadriga back to Venice were more than a little embarrassed at themselves for not sending it back to the only place they knew positively that it actually came from. Anyway, the Floating City is naturally Venice whilst the New Rome, we think, is a dig at Napoleon."

"Nobody's above a good dig it seems," Russo commented.

"Nope. And with Napoleon just defeated and jailed after referencing his Paris as the New Rome we think the theory stands up."

Alicia racked her memory. " 'Undivided as Lysippos intended'. That's pretty clear."

"It is," Crouch broke back in with a smile. "Lysippos built these pieces to complement each other. Spectacle and strength. The show and the unseen power at its back. They were never meant to be parted."

"So maybe they never were," Healey said. "And we head back to St. Mark's Basilica."

"Maybe." Crouch nodded. "The next two lines are more references to the pieces' meaning. What they signify to each other. The quadriga—"

"Wait." Healey broke in, waving an arm and sidestepping a bungling tourist. "What is a quadriga anyway? I missed that bit."

"A quadriga is four horses. Four horsepower. It was pretty quick back in the day."

Alicia laughed. "Fourth century BCE? I'll bet."

"Now," Caitlyn took up the metaphorical reins, "is where it gets interesting. The final stanza tells us where the Hercules is currently, or at least where it was taken after 1815. And looking at the big picture, that's just a moment ago in history. It says 'then sundered materially but never in spirit'. This points to the very real possibility that the pieces were parted. The Horses sent to Venice, the Hercules . . ."

"But why?" Russo asked.

"There must have been a very good reason. The people who wrote the congress clearly knew the pieces were meant to stay together."

"And where?" Alicia asked.

"Read the rest of the verse. What do you think?"

"By the Pillars of Hercules," Alicia recalled. "A part of the soil. Hiding among New Arches envisioned. To the victor the spoils."

"This is where we falter," Crouch admitted. "I've never heard of the Pillars of Hercules or the New Arches. And 'to the victor the spoils' seems almost to be a challenge. More like the hunt, a riddle-master saying—if you find it it's yours."

Caitlyn stared into the middle distance. "Well, I do know that the Pillars of Hercules are two promontories at the Strait of Gibraltar. One of them is the actual Rock of Gibraltar."

"Lots of, um, toffs out that way," Russo said. "I don't think we'd fit in."

"I know of the Rock of Gibraltar," Crouch said. "Of course. But I didn't realize the Pillar of Hercules connection."

"And Napoleon's activities in the Med are well documented," Caitlyn added. "My only problem is the quote we found from Napoleon: 'I have *found* the Pillars of Hercules. That doesn't quite fit."

"All right." Crouch stored that away for later perusal. "Let's concentrate on the New Arches reference for a bit. We'll revisit the Pillars of Hercules later."

"Wasn't the Arc de Triomphe built after the Arc du Carrousel?" Alicia asked.

"Yes, but they were designed and begun at the same time. You think 'arches' refers to the triumphal arches of Paris?"

"Or Rome." Alicia shrugged. "Wasn't that where arches first started off?"

"Ancient Rome, yes," Crouch replied quietly, clearly thinking hard. "As I mentioned there's an Arch of Constantine in Rome."

Healey jerked alert, ready to go. Alicia waved him down. "Relax, boy. We're just guesstimating here."

"Constantine just doesn't fit," Caitlyn said. "Yes, he built Constantinople but the congress washes right over the history around Constantinople and the Hippodrome."

Crouch agreed. "All Roman arches are old," he said. "Dating, I think from around the first century BCE onwards."

"And they meant 'envisioned' back in 1815." Alicia said. "That means they hadn't been built yet."

Crouch shook his head. "But that doesn't fit either. Nobody would build a triumphal arch just to hide the Hercules. They'd secrete it in a quiet place they already have. I mean, the Hippodrome was already there. So was the Golden Palace and St. Mark's Basilica. Even the Arc du Carrousel was built to commemorate Napoleon's victories."

"So maybe the arches weren't built just for the Hercules," Alicia shrugged, "but agreed at the secret congress to be utilized later in some way."

Caitlyn stared at Crouch. "Something you just said." She creased her brow. "Niggles at me. About Napoleon and his victories. I don't . . ." she broke off, deep in thought.

"So where does all that leave us?" Russo grumbled, staring around at the erratic flows of tourists, the drifting crisp packets and empty coffee cups, the local cops trying their best to look friendly on every street corner, the ever-present, all-seeing monuments that marked eras long since absent from the world.

"Well, it leaves us with plenty to think about," Crouch said a little grumpily. "And that's why we're here."

"Not me." Alicia looked like a caged lion. "I'm here for the mayhem. I'm just dying for some lout to bump into me so I can tear his head off."

"Frustrated?" Russo enquired with a little smirk.

"I may be the worst woman here," Alicia said with a tight, haughty smile. "But I'm still the best man."

Crouch started walking away from the arch, pulling the team with him. "Do we know of any arches built after 1815?"

Alicia turned to Caitlyn. "Geek?"

The ex-MI5 agent looked flustered. "Sorry, I was . . . lost for a moment there. I'm sure the answer is staring us right in the face."

"No," Alicia said drily. "That's me. And I'm not hiding any Hercules."

"It's not that." Caitlyn said, oblivious to the sarcasm. "I'm thinking Napoleon was defeated. The Hercules and to some extent the quadriga always seem to have been spoils of war. So who defeated Napoleon?"

Crouch stopped very quickly. "Field Marshal Arthur Wellesley at the battle of Waterloo," he said. "Better known as the Duke of Wellington."

"And you're saying the British built an arch in acknowledgement of that?" Alicia asked.

"No." Caitlyn flicked rapidly at her Kindle Fire. "We built two. The first design was based on the Arch of Constantine," she breathed rapidly. "and wow . . . the Arc de Triomphe du Carrousel. The second, complete with quadriga, was also built to commemorate Britain's victories in the Napoleonic Wars."

The team stared at each other, mesmerized by Caityln's words, astonished at the breakthrough.

"Which arches?" Crouch asked. "Don't tell me—"

Caitlyn nodded. "You got it. The most obvious ones in plain sight. The first is Marble Arch, the second is Wellington Arch."

TWENTY SEVEN

Alicia watched as the expression on Crouch's face changed from incredulity to hope and determination.

"By the Pillars of Hercules. A part of the soil," he said. "But what of the last line—to the victor the spoils. Wait . . ." He palmed his head, the blow audible to all. "Of course. It's not referring to those hunting the Hercules, it's referring solely to Wellington. To the victor the spoils. He claimed it."

"Time to gen up on our British history," Alicia said. "Where did Wellington—"

At that moment her text-message tone went off. A message from Beau—*get ready*.

That can't be good.

A few seconds later Crouch's cell rang. He held up a hand as he answered. "Yes?"

Again, many guises warped his features from one emotion to the next. "Now?" he asked. "Here? Where?"

Alicia didn't like the sound of it, and liked waiting to hear the forthcoming revelation even less. The connection between Beau's text and Crouch's call didn't escape her. Crouch let out a long sigh and held the phone's speaker against his chest.

"I have intel that Riley is here in Paris," he said. "I also have a locality. We could hit him whilst he's unprepared."

Alicia saw the man's turmoil. They all sensed how close they were to the prize, yet here was an opportunity to rid themselves of a new and extremely deadly disease.

"Do it," she said. "It's worth the time and effort."

Russo grumbled in agreement. Crouch was already nodding. Quickly, he thanked the person on the other end of the phone, took a few notes and then ended the call.

"Out of interest." Alicia raised her chin. "Who was that?"

Crouch eyed her keenly. "I think you already know."

Alicia couldn't hide her surprise. "Now that's a shocker."

"I can't explain now but I will explain later. When all this is over."

"Can't?" Russo repeated in bewilderment. "Explain? Over? What the hell are you two talking about?"

Couch brandished a small piece of paper. "Doesn't matter now," he said. "We have a job to do,"

Alicia watched Crouch work his magic, contacting Armand Argento at Interpol and finding a local contact that would be willing to help with weapons. It helped that Interpol was located not too far away and that Argento knew Crouch inside out. The two had worked together more times than either cared to remember down the years.

Within an hour, by way of a hastily commandeered governmental van, they were approaching the address Crouch's mystery caller had provided.

A petite abandoned train station stood atop a small bridge above a fully-functioning railway line, just ten meters from the entrance to a long tunnel. The station was painted white and black, a classic destination for graffiti artists, and still had all its windows intact and sparkling clean, its roof whole and free of moss and its drainpipes freshly painted. The small staircase that ran up to its door, however, was railed off both to the sides and above. Small trees had begun to grow along its length. Alicia saw now that Riley's men had broken the locks on the gate and made their way up the stairs and into the station. It was a perfect hiding place, central, clean and so long as they were careful, anonymous.

How had Beau . . . ?

She didn't want to know. Beauregard had his sinuous ways

and his sneaky secrets. Alicia preferred not to dig too deep. One thing was certain—she could never hope to worm her way into the heart of a deadly, global secret sect like the Pythians. All glory to Beauregard for doing so.

The team crept along the embankment, sticking to the top where the hedges were overgrown and offered maximum concealment. Crouch pointed out there was no second-guessing Daniel Riley, the man made everything up as he went along and rarely acted the same way twice. His skills are his unpredictabilities, Crouch told them. His security his craziness. His strength his depravities. Do not expect mercy nor surety from this man.

Alicia trod lightly, guns in both her hands. One held a standard Glock, the other a HK machine pistol, both fully loaded. Other weapons were concealed about her person. The team could not know how many men Riley had recruited, though their "informant" had mentioned "more than a dozen". Alicia was happy to be working proactively against him at last. No more running.

Ahead, the station stood atop the graffiti-covered bridge, gleaming in the sunlight. Alicia could see heads bobbing through the windows. She signaled Crouch.

"Enemy's at home."

"Good."

Together, they advanced. No sentries appeared to have been placed, but Alicia knew there would be no access to the station except through the railed off staircase. Even if they could gain the roof unseen the noise would alert those inside. Crouch bent down, crawling as close as he dared, and raised high-powered binoculars to his eyes.

"Target confirmed," he said. "I see Riley and . . . eight more men."

At that moment a train approached, clattering hard down the rusted tracks before passing under the bridge and disappearing into the long tunnel. Alicia watched the carriages flash past, their seats full of unsuspecting passengers. The noise made Riley's mercs glance out the window. Crouch could have waited; he could have crept closer; he could even have pinned the mercs down. But instead, probably still unsettled by the appearance of an old nemesis, he unloaded his machine pistol into the train station. Even Alicia yelled in alarm, but by then the blood was already flowing.

Mercs tumbled left and right and sheets of glass rained from the windows down onto the track. Alicia had a wild, displaced thought: Good job it wasn't leaves! and crabbed forward. Men approached the frame, bodies revealed, and she made them pay the price. Quickly, she half ran down the embankment to the train tracks, knowing the carriages thundered along at seven minute intervals.

Mercs leapt out of the windows, landing on the embankment and trying to steady their feet. One brushed by her as he landed, his momentum forcing her to her knees. Russo was at her side, snapping the unfortunate's neck and hurling him aside.

Healey bounded like a spring lamb ahead, happy to be unleashed. A man came at him head-on. Healey upended his machine pistol into his chin, poleaxing him faster than thought. Bullets chewed up the dirt at his feet.

Alicia aimed her own weapon up at the smashed windows above. The mercs were lining the opening, four of them with smirks on their faces. Alicia dived aside. As she did so bullets ripped across the mercs' chests, fired from Crouch and Caitlyn's direction. Two dropped outside, two inside, and then two more jumped out. Alicia met the first as soon as he landed, dodging a wild swing. First she broke ribs, then a knee and finally a neck.

No mercy. These people had already fired on civilians.

The second man landed. Alicia disarmed him, taking an elbow to the cheekbone for her trouble. Pain flashed at the center of her brain. More mercs were appearing now from the fringes of the battle, as if they'd been ensconced in some other hiding place. Alicia saw Riley. Crouch's weapon barked faster. A merc tumbled down the uneven slope. There was suddenly the rumble and clank of an approaching train. Alicia gripped her opponent by the throat, batted away his strong arms, and then hurled him against the flashing carriage. The body bounced and flopped and then lay still, broken.

Two men leaped onto her. Alicia fell under their onslaught, now finding herself rolling unstoppably toward the reverberating carriages. She dug her fingers hard into the grass, but came up only with soil. As she made one more revolution, her arms held out protectively before her, the last carriage raced past. Alicia bounced onto the empty track, the solid rails jarring her spine.

One of the pursuing mercs grinned. "Bet that hurt, bitch."

Alicia jumped to her feet. "Let's see you back that comment up."

The merc checked briefly to make sure his colleague was beside him and then pounced. Alicia executed a half-circle turn, brushing off his back, then smashed the other merc between the eyes with a stiff arm. As he blinked Alicia spun again, now facing the first merc.

"Still full of wind and piss, boy?"

The man yelled a challenge and ran at her. Alicia jumped on the spot, her front kick crashing into his chest, breaking bone. Still he came. Alicia skipped aside, found her Glock in the grass and sent both men to deal with the Devil.

Above, a frantic melee had broken out. Riley was at the center of a group that included three mercs, Russo and Healey. Two more mercs darted at the fringes, causing Russo major problems. Crouch was running full-pelt to join them.

Alicia saw this was the end. There were no more mercenaries in hiding. Digging deep, she ran up the embankment to join the fray, heading straight for the two mercs who were plaguing Russo. Below, another train clattered on by, its occupants probably raising the alarm by now even if the previous ones hadn't. Alicia tossed her empty pistol at one merc, bringing her HK to bear on the other. The barrel spat. The merc threw himself aside, caught only by one bullet in the right arm. It wasn't enough. Alicia saw the gritted teeth, the determined stare and knew she was up against a seasoned killer. His own gun was now aimed at her, finger tugging at the trigger. Blood suddenly gouted from his chest, the gun firing off, but the bullets flew wild. Crouch pounded in alongside, red in the face and mad as hell.

"Riley!"

The mercs were beginning to thin out. Russo took another down, but Healey took a heavy blow to the head that sent him spinning to the ground. Alicia immediately remembered his possible head trauma from the previous explosion and berated herself. Should have shielded him. Again, the generally out-of-character thought unnerved her. *What am I becoming?*

She sprang across to him, felling a merc on the way much to his sudden shock. Healey was groaning on the grass, his body draped half over the top of the steep slope. A merc stood over him with a knife.

"Hey."

Spinning fast, the man slashed wide. Alicia anticipated it, ducked under and came up with a throat jab. Behind her shots still rang out. As she danced from side to side she saw Crouch engage Riley. Only three mercs remained at his side. The man who couldn't be captured, it seemed, was about to go down hard.

Alicia evaded the knife again, jumping between Healey's

legs and then over his head. Crouch traded blows with Riley, the first time she could actually remember seeing her boss in a fist fight.

Not good.

Riley was a crazy, seasoned fighter. What the hell was Crouch thinking? Alicia almost missed her opponent's feint and thrust, so focused on Crouch's battle was she. The blade nicked her stab vest and ricocheted across her arm, drawing a line of blood through the thick black sleeve. As soon as the man stood back to admire his handiwork and affect a little grin Alicia moved faster than he could comprehend. Before the intense fact that he was actually dead reached his brain he was flat out on the floor.

Alicia bent over to check on Healey. "You okay, you bloody idiot?"

"Yeah," Healey gasped, high-pitched. "It's all good."

"Stay there."

She turned, scooped up the dead man's knife and headed toward Crouch. Riley already seemed to be on top of the skirmish, bloodying her boss's face with callused knuckles. Alicia saw the stance and actions of a man who engaged in fist fights for fun. A bare-knuckle boxer. Riley was enjoying himself. And that insight too attested to his craziness—his men were dropping faster than trees in the Amazon.

Russo smashed enormous arms onto a merc's scalp, groaning in pain but never flinching. Alicia slid by. Riley saw her approach and immediately pushed Crouch aside. Dropping his hands by his sides he thrust his chest out.

"Take yer best shot, babe."

Alicia couldn't stop a snigger. "Are you for real?"

"He's stalling. Take him out, Alicia," Crouch gasped. "Now!"

She fingered the hilt of the knife. "Turn around and hold your arms out," she said. "You're beaten."

"Never."

Riley ran at her, taking the knife in the stomach but succeeding in knocking her off her feet. As she fell backward she heard the sound of an oncoming train. Riley's fleeing feet never faltered. He battered Russo aside, even the living mountain momentarily destabilized. Russo fell to one knee, aghast.

Riley ran as if pursued by demons, and perhaps he was. The train barreled down the tracks, its horn blowing. At first Alicia thought he was about to throw himself at the train rather than be taken alive, but then she saw.

The bastard had timed it to the millisecond.

He couldn't plan for lateness, but he'd certainly spent enough time here to plan for punctuality. Alicia could only stare as Riley sprinted hard, looking for all the world as if he was about to smash to pieces against the front of the train, then hurled himself across the tracks. A split-instant later the train swept by. Riley raced up the other embankment, gaining the top in seconds.

Crouch shouted for a gun. Alicia cast around, seeing nothing. Russo continued his collapse and shoveled up a Glock between both hands, throwing it over to Crouch.

"Bollocks!" their leader swore. "You should have taken the bloody shot. Look at me!"

Already, his face was swollen, one eye swelling. Riley didn't hang around over the other side. Already, he was disappearing around the far edge of the abandoned station. Alicia made to chase after him as the train passed.

A shot rang out, stunning Alicia. A puff of mortar exploded beside Riley's right ear, making him stumble. Alicia turned to see Caitlyn holding a rifle.

"Good try," she said. "Now let's go get him."

"Forget it," Crouch said. "Bastard will already have had an escape route planned. Three or four even. He's a part of the landscape."

"But he's severely debilitated," Caitlyn said, coming up now. "Alone. Badly wounded. He won't last long."

Crouch closed his eyes tightly. "You don't understand. Riley has as many contacts as I do, only all his are bad. He'll survive. And he'll be back. Maybe alone, but even that's a vicious prospect."

Alicia squinted over at Healey. The young man was sitting up, listening. "Well," she said. "What say we gather up our wounded and our motivation and get on a plane to London?"

"I say let's just get the hell outta Paris," Russo mumbled, still on his knees.

"Need a hand, Robby?"

"No I friggin' don't."

"Haven't seen you knocked over before."

"Shut it."

Crouch placed tentative hands on his face. "How do I look?"

"My first thought is pepperoni pizza," Alicia said graciously. "But no. No. Seriously, it's not that bad. The facial swelling will ease in an hour or two. The eye—a bit longer."

"Think I'll survive passport control?"

"Meh. Just bribe 'em."

"So what are we waiting for? London's calling."

TWENTY EIGHT

Crouch tried to force his mind away from Riley and their checkered past by concentrating on their unfolding treasure hunt. The Hercules Tarentum had evidently been designed alongside Lysippos' Horses and had remained almost undivided throughout history. And once Napoleon had been defeated at Waterloo, clearing the way for the Horses to be returned to Venice, who would stand in the way of the victor claiming the spoils?

Admittedly, Crouch didn't know an awful lot about the Duke of Wellington. The enormous arch that sat at the center of Hyde Park Corner was named after him and the house just across the road—Apsley House—had been his residence. With an address of Number One, London it was clear how high in esteem the British had held him. But, standing at the heart of London and a true British Heritage site, what did it have to do with Hercules and Napoleon? Maybe nothing . . . the arches were still their main focus. It would take much further delving but Crouch did know that the Wellington and Marble arches had been moved sometime in their history and that the foremost had been designed as some kind of grand entrance to London.

And of course, there was a quadriga on top—a four-horse chariot.

With the plane in the air, Crouch and his compatriots found themselves drifting. Exhausted through battle and city-hopping and mind-draining deliberations they fell into deep, dream-filled sleep. Crouch achieved no such release. After dozing for a few minutes he came wide awake, agitated by memories he had thought long dead and buried.

Following the bombing in India, Riley had once again dropped off the grid, leaving Crouch with nothing beyond infinite scenes of horror. Trying to reconcile that night with the man he had previously liked and worried over took years, and even then doubts remained. Not excusable, but had Riley acted under duress? Was a terrorist cell holding someone he loved, someone Riley had never disclosed? Crouch didn't see Riley again for many years after that night but heard about his further exploits through the interdepartmental grapevine. Riley always remained high on the watch list but never again came to the in-field attention of the SAS.

Now Crouch doubted himself. What the hell had he been doing allowing this man to roam free all these years? Should I have pushed it? Certain terrorists needed making an example of—Riley was surely one of those.

Crouch tore his mind back to the present as their pilot announced the descent into London. Focusing again on the arches he thought that the links were good, the final resting place of the Hercules close at hand. If these treasures continually passed into the hands of conquering leaders— which history said they did—then the Hercules would still be somewhere in London. The Duke of Wellington's descendants would never give up such a magnificent treasure. And to think of all the many thousands who passed through those arches every single day . . .

Crouch felt a tremor of excitement, pushed all thoughts of Riley and Kenzie aside, and watched the descent into London City Airport.

TWENTY NINE

Kenzie wondered silently as to the perils of folly. She had found it relatively easy tracking Crouch to France, but after the fiasco back in Vienna she'd had to quell a little revolt. The men of her inner circle helped, those who survived, and she put her survival down to the ruthlessness with which she had subdued the rebels.

Pacing a hotel room, she waited for news.

Windows looked out across the Seine to the Eiffel Tower, the view not even a small distraction for Kenzie. She lived to acquire wealth and desirable objects, not to stare at them. Since arriving in France she had recruited more men, and another to listen to the newcomers' conversations, a little mole. It was her way. She kept order and she kept her life. Everything was good.

Except for Crouch and his little band of brothers.

In a normal world they might even elude her, but this was not normal, this was her world. Kenzie had kept it quiet even among her inner circle, but one of the men she employed was a previous Ninth Division operative. Battered, bruised and left for dead in the ruins of the old HQ he had risen disgruntled, resentful, and sought out some extreme alternative employment. After bumbling around for several months he had been brought to her attention. Kenzie recognized the potential and snapped him up in a minute—ex-government employees always came in useful.

Three men shared the hotel room with her, two of the three remaining members of her inner circle and the Ninth Division traitor—Jaden Sheppard. The latter was privy to several of Michael Crouch's lines of contact and was monitoring them all.

"London," Sheppard told her. "We couldn't find them in France but I know where they will be in London."

Kenzie stared sightlessly out of the window. "When? Are they already in the air?"

Sheppard nodded. "Even if we left right now we'd be two hours behind them."

"Luckily," she stared hard at him, "I have people in London. Ancient relics are big business among the city's greedy bankers and businessmen. Crouch can't have found his treasure yet . . ." she tailed off, her mind flicking back through the years and to the events that had led her to this. Once a loyal operative of Mossad she broke hard and went rogue when an op went wrong. The fallout had killed a man she loved and, later, her family. At twenty eight she had seen the faults inherent in government, officials on the take, and people who should be looking out for her, mentors, superiors, equals, reveling in all their squalid dishonesties. Breaking from her heart to her brain she made the decision to work only for herself and to never trust one single person ever again.

There was a knock at the door, an intrusion. One of her acolytes rose, checked through the peep-hole, and opened it. Her missing inner-circle member entered looking a bit red in the face.

"Everything okay?" Kenzie asked.

"Aye," the rough-looking Scotsman growled. "Everything's great. Just a wee problem to sort, that's all."

"More dissension among the ranks?"

"You got it, Kenzie. New boy by the name of Gilmore. Thinks he's gonna be running the whole crew soon enough, he does."

"Of course. There's always one. Always. Did you make an example of him?"

"Not yet. Thought I'd check with you first. Don't wanna run afoul of that blade ye always keep handy."

Kenzie eyed the shining, curved blade close at hand. The weapon gave her power over all aspects of her life—it was a deterrent, a life-giver, a confidence restorer and a menacing threat. It was her backbone in life, her perversion in passion, her twisted child.

The katana was all. It should be worshipped. Knowing what would happen she reached out and held it high, expecting her men to bow their heads and smiling when they did so.

"Make arrangements to fly straight to London," she said. "And let Gilmore run his mouth for now. We'll deal with him in the UK and it'll hit any would-be insurgents all the harder."

The Scotsman looked happy, a rare event outside payday. The thought made her think of the very near future when they caught Crouch in the act of uncovering millions of dollars worth of riches. It made her think of the worship, respect and loyalty it would implant into her men. It made her think of other things she could aspire to do outside this world of backstabbers and thieves.

It made her dream. She sliced the katana through a series of complicated moves.

The future was at her doorstep. All she had to do was cross the threshold.

THIRTY

London basked in shameful sunshine, ensuring the streets were filled with tourists and locals, businessmen out for brief walks and office workers heading for the closest Pret or Eat or any number of thousands of small lunchtime eateries. Traffic clogged the roads as much as people jammed the walkways, its roar and hum and constant throb the beating heart of the thriving city. Alicia strode ahead, exiting the underground station of Marble Arch and stopping briefly to get her bearings. Humanity flowed around her.

"That way." Crouch pointed and she saw the ceremonial arch briefly to their right before it was obscured by several passing double-decker buses. The team set off and Russo fell in alongside.

"Sure hope the boss has a plan. It's not like a supposed treasure that has remained hidden all these years is gonna jump up through a trapdoor somewhere."

Alicia shrugged. "Stranger things have happened."

"Umm, for instance?"

"Well, you not fancying a roll in the sack with me for a start."

"You think that's strange? Boy, do you have an odd view of the world."

"Sure I do. You're right, I do have an odd view of the world, but that's what makes me me."

"I think sometimes it's all an act."

Alicia gave neutral laugh. "When? And why?"

"When you want to distract somebody from discovering the real you."

"Shit, Russo, what are you? A closet psychiatrist?"

"I studied psychology in college."

"No way! Do not tell me you're another freakin' geek too."

"Nah. I'm fucking a little with you. I dropped out of college after starting my degree. Six months. Pissed the hell outta my folks."

"Joined the Army? I was there at sixteen and have been running ever since. Hey, look at us—both survived this far."

"And for much longer."

"Statistics state we don't live long enough for this to be the right way, Russo. Shouldn't it be about having fun? You know—one life, live it."

They paused at a set of traffic lights that would let them cross the busy junction at Edgware Road to reach Marble Arch. Russo nudged Alicia. "I thought we were having fun."

"I guess we are, but it's all going to fall apart," Alicia said seriously.

"Ah. Your breakdown. It doesn't have to be so hard."

"If I don't fall hard I doubt that I'll get back up."

Russo hushed as they crossed the road in front of traffic that was straining at the leash. Ahead, the arch and the area around it sat waiting. Crouch and Caitlyn were striding forward, already scanning the structure as if the Hercules might mysteriously and suddenly be revealed. Healey stayed close to Caitlyn as if appreciating her energy and cheerfulness.

Alicia stopped before the white-colored arch, gazing up toward its uppermost reaches. Bright blue skies dazzled her eyes. The top was flat, no quadriga or any other statues sat up there. Four thick columns stood across its width and the only markings she could see were several carvings above the gates. The gates themselves were open wide, admitting the masses. Smaller gates stood inside archways to either side. After a while Crouch suggested they walk through to the other side.

"Not sure what I expected," he said. "I realize we need more in-depth research but it's always good to see your current nemesis in the flesh."

The other side of Marble Arch was as ornate and unremarkable as the first. The carvings did not reveal Hercules, or even a horse, although some did suggest a Roman flavor. It was Caitlyn who opted to form a new plan.

"Over there," she pointed across Park Lane, "is a small pub with free Wi-Fi." She squinted. "Let's hit the keys and also see if there's a way to gain entry to these arches. We'll check their history. Their provenance. Those who are associated with them. Something has to turn up."

Crouch nodded. "As ever your enthusiasm is our guide."

The pub appeared busy from the outside; all the small, unsteady tables were crowded with people enjoying loud conversations, each one trying to outdo the next, but once inside the shaded interior Alicia found they had their pick of tables. Crouch chose a semi-circle booth in the far corner and they were soon comfortably seated with waters and sodas in hand and nibbles on the way. This was about as close to normality as Alicia ever came and it made her slightly uncomfortable.

"Let's get on with it," she said. "I don't exactly feel safe here."

Russo peered at her. "In that odd way of yours I know exactly what you mean. Give me a dark alleyway, an Uzi and a set of night goggles any day."

Alicia raised her glass in salute. "To the simple pleasures of hunting desperados and gangsters."

Russo clinked. "And to destroying them all."

Healey joined in at the last moment, clinking hard. Caitlyn had Crouch's attention further around the highly polished table. "So, Marble Arch was actually designed to be the state entrance to the three-sided courtyard at the newly rebuilt

Buckingham Palace. Clearly, a structure given great honor. It stood there until 1851 when it was relocated here."

Crouch tapped at the screen. "This is interesting. Many sculptures and friezes were made for the arch which subsequently were never used. A frieze of Waterloo and the Nelson panels were later used at Buckingham Palace. Others were sent to the National Gallery and Trafalgar Square. Again, based on the Arch of Constantine it commemorated the Duke of Wellington's victories against Napoleon. It is hollow," he stressed excitedly, then looked disappointed. "Three rooms inside were used as a police station until 1968."

Alicia sipped her water. "That doesn't rule out the possibility of more rooms."

"No, but it's so small. There would be no easy way to view a statue inside so what's the point? The inner rooms are public knowledge too. And it's situated at the heart of a large traffic island."

"As is Wellington Arch," Caitlyn pointed out. "Why would they do that?"

"A good question," Crouch said. "Does it say why they moved the arch away from Buckingham Palace?"

Caitlyn flicked through various pages. "Not conclusively and not officially. Another dead end. They built a new east range on Buck Palace which today is the public façade, helping to shield the inner façades from view."

"These people just love creating conspiracy theories," Healey said with a grin.

"Unnecessarily," Crouch agreed. "Through all their pomp and circumstance. But I do wonder about their positioning of Marble Arch . . ."

Alicia agreed. "So incongruous," she said. "And hard to reach for many."

Food arrived and talk halted for a while. Caitlyn flicked around her tablet as they ate, but came up with little else.

When they were done Crouch proposed they walk down Park Lane to Hyde Park Corner and take a look at the second triumphal arch. The trip was uneventful, though noisy, and resplendent with old hotels and frontages, an odd petrol station built on a steep slope and several underground parking garages. Beyond the Park Lane Hilton the road curved toward the traffic lights that looked over Hyde Park Corner.

Alicia followed her colleagues down the long, prominent road and then down the steps that led to the underpass, thinking all the while of their quest, their enemies, her future and her few real friends. Beauregard was also on her mind— the ally who might be an adversary or might be about to switch or . . . shit, who the hell knew who the Frenchman really was?

Along the underpass they passed two homeless men wrapped in blankets, one conversing with a tourist about the problems faced by vagrants—how the government just refused to help them because they were too interested in housing immigrants.

It made some sense to Alicia. There was no money in helping the destitute.

She dropped money into an upturned hat, then found herself traversing a tiled passage on which several caricatures of the Duke of Wellington were displayed. Crouch stopped to view them but said nothing. Caitlyn went ahead with Healey, the two enjoying a private conversation and leaning into one another. As Alicia climbed and then reached the top of the steps the Wellington Arch came into sight to her left.

It reminded her of the Arc du Carrousel, though its façade was nowhere near as ornate. It stood grand, stunning, empowering, an epic commemoration to victory, to triumph. Surmounting it was the grand quadriga, the original vision of its designer, a colossal bronze depicting Nike, the Winged Goddess of Victory, descending to the Chariot of War. The largest bronze sculpture in all of Europe. To Alicia it evoked feelings of wonder, but they were mixed with disquiet. The memorial to her right, the Royal Artillery Memorial with its list of many names was far more meaningful to her.

"It's also hollow," Crouch told them. "There's a museum inside, fairly big, but nothing more." He turned on the spot, taking in the surrounds, the sunlight sparkling off the windows of Apsley House—the residence of the Duke of Wellington—the traffic peeling around Hyde Park Corner and vanishing up Piccadilly toward the Ritz and down Pall Mall toward Buckingham Palace.

"This feels . . . right," he said. "How many people standing on the grass here or passing under this arch might guess a priceless treasure lies somewhere about? How many privileged people mock their ignorance?"

"But where could it be?" Caitlyn said. "I see nothing useful."

"Nor would you. It is time we dug around a bit more. There's the treasure of a lifetime lying around London's busy streets, my friends, I'm sure of it. And even more—I'm sure that we're going to find it."

THIRTY ONE

Alicia later found herself inside yet another disconcerting place—a public restaurant just off Park Lane. The bar area was busy, the tables full, the noise tremendous. The stage at the far end was inviting those couples who wished to dance, the queue outside stretching around the corner. The Gold Team had been settled for a while, and were determined to remain until they'd shed some light on their current mystery.

Alicia picked at her food, a juicy steak salad. The meat was delicious, the greens splattered with some nasty acidic sauce. As she contemplated tracking down the person who'd decided the extra dressing was appropriate a familiar face approached through the throng that separated their table from the front door.

Kenzie.

Alicia half rose, the fork gripped in her hand.

Kenzie laughed as she approached, holding both hands open and giving a quick twirl to show she wasn't armed. The skintight black jeans and high, floaty white blouse she wore publicized that not even a cellphone was hidden on her body.

"Love the jeans," Alicia said. "But I'd work out more, love. Lose some of the fat on that ass." As she spoke Alicia's eyes roved the restaurant. Every face, every body was skimmed. No obvious threats registered.

Kenzie looked a little outraged. "I didn't come here to swop insults, bitch, I came here to offer you a deal."

The lithe-bodied, black-haired woman squeezed in next to Healey. Caitlyn gave her an obvious warning look but she only chuckled. "Steak looks good," she said, sliding the plate from under Healey's nose. "Do you mind?"

Healey gestured helplessly and glided over the leather to Caitlyn's side. Kenzie picked up his knife and fork, then cut and skewered a large piece of rib eye. As she chewed she eyed both Alicia and Crouch.

Silence blanketed the table. Not even the noisy patrons nor the loud music penetrated their bubble. Crouch had an odd look on his face—one of fear mixed with disbelief and it was then that Alicia remembered the events that transpired during his old, original encounter with Daniel Riley.

He was intersecting the two, worrying over something that Kenzie—despite her maliciousness—would never do. Kenzie wanted to retire wealthy, not spend the rest of her days being hunted.

"Deal?" Alicia prompted. "Spit it out."

"I'd rather swallow, thank you." Kenzie still chewed the lump, cheeks working hard.

"Yeah, why doesn't that surprise me?"

Kenzie coughed, looking sick. "Oh, you certainly know how to put a girl off her food."

Alicia gestured toward the dance floor. "Wanna dance?"

"Are you serious?"

"You got something to say you better whisper it in my ear. We're already too exposed out here."

Kenzie watched the dancers. "Then let's go."

Alicia rose, slipped out from behind the table and held out a hand. Without missing a beat Kenzie took it and the two women walked together to the dance floor. At her back Alicia heard Healey's strangled excuse as Caitlyn rebuked him for staring too hard. In reality the move isolated Kenzie even more, cemented the knowledge that she had no backup and put her solely in Alicia's hands. That she had accepted was more telling to Alicia than any amount of words.

"So," she placed her hands on Kenzie's hips and started to

move to the music, "what debauchery do you have in mind?"

Kenzie's eyes were centimeters away. "A deal. You help me out with half of the treasure and I help you with Daniel Riley."

"And if not?"

"I'll have every available merc for five hundred miles at your throats."

They moved among the other dancers, the music alive with rhythm and power, the beat that stirred Alicia's blood.

She placed her lips close to Kenzie's left ear. "You ever heard of Dino Rock?"

"Uh, no."

"It's just a reference to old rock music. But I have a friend who likes to quote it, at least he used to before one of his best friends died. I'm reminded of a line now, something like—do you do more than dance?"

Kenzie pushed away at the sight of Alicia's smiling, knowing eyes. "Shit, stop trying to freak me out. You already have me off balance. Are we dealing or not?"

Alicia pulled Kenzie in tight. "What do you know of Daniel Riley?"

"I don't know his past," Kenzie admitted. "Or how he relates to you. But I do know he survived France and that he's now in London. Anything beyond that you're going to have to help me out first."

"Oh, I'll help you out." Alicia swung Kenzie around and marched her through the throng. "If I see you again it won't be so pleasant."

"When I see you again it will be my blade that gets close to you, not my body."

Alicia pushed her toward the exit and gave her a swat. "Remember. Start hitting that gym."

Crouch was half on his feet but Alicia waved him back down. "She's bluffing," she said as she returned to her meal. "Wants to give us Riley info in exchange for the treasure.

Forget her—what have you guys learned?"

Caitlyn spoke rapidly, probably wanting to regain Healey's full attention, "London's two triumphal arches, Wellington and Marble, have remarkably parallel histories. Both were designed and built as great entrances to Buckingham Palace and to commemorate victory over Napoleon. Both were later moved to different positions and both were marooned on large traffic islands. The Wellington Arch is indeed hollow and houses a museum though it too housed a police station until 1992."

"The statue simply can't he housed in the arches," Crouch told her. "Now that we've seen them in the flesh, they're too public. That leaves—"

"Beneath?" she ventured.

"Well, I was going to say 'a different location that's somehow tied to the arches'. But . . ." he tailed off, thoughtful.

"You'd have a major problem," Healey said. "There's more than a fair chance the underground runs under Hyde Park Corner."

"A problem," Crouch said carefully. "Or an opportunity."

"When was the underground built?" Healey asked.

"That doesn't matter," Crouch said. "The statue can clearly be moved quite easily if you know how and have the appropriate wherewithal. It could have had multiple locations during its time here."

"We need to revisit both arches and check for tunnels," Alicia said. "But in the meantime I suggest we get out of here. Kenzie isn't as crazy as Riley but she's still a bloody loon."

"And pissed off," Crouch agreed. He signaled for and settled the bill. The team rose and stretched, then filed out of the restaurant, feeling the tepid air breezing down London's busy streets. The nightlife was well and truly abuzz on such a balmy night in the capital. Alicia saw groups standing outside pubs with beers in hand, lining the streets; parents carrying sleepy children whilst they pushed empty strollers; stylishly dressed ladies prancing by on high heels, weighed down by many bags sporting the names Gucci, Harrods and French Connection. She watched the crowds.

"We should mingle," she said. "And find a hotel."

"There's always The Ritz." Crouch indicated a golden spectacle further up Piccadilly.

Alicia laughed. "Yeah, right. We'll all feel right at home there. I was thinking something a little less snobby."

Crouch cast his eye down toward Hyde Park Corner and the Wellington Arch. "Well, there's always Knightsbridge—"

And then Kenzie was back, full in their faces, with an unpleasant crowd of mercenaries at her side.

"Go get 'em boys."

Alicia moved faster. The lag between spotting Kenzie, analyzing her superiority in numbers, and spotting an escape route was entirely non-existent. The big red double-decker had pulled up three minutes ago to disgorge its passengers and registered immediately on her radar. Now, as the last person jumped off and others prepared to board she raced forward to the edge of the curb.

"Get back!" she cried. "Away from the bus!"

A large youth with spiky hair proceeded to quickly guffaw and clown his way to a set of bruised testicles and was left groaning on the floor. His hard-learned lesson dissuaded most of the others. Alicia dragged the driver clear as Crouch pulled Caitlyn up the low step. The driver then proved useful as a projectile to dissuade the first merc, Alicia yelling sorry in his wake. Russo and Healey reached the bus as Crouch slid behind the wheel, revving hard. Alicia threw the driver's ragged backpack at the merc closest to Russo, sending him reeling. Healey jumped up.

Crouch engaged the gears and floored the gas pedal. Russo's face took on a look of panic as he ran. A merc grabbed his throat from behind only to be swatted aside like a fruit fly. Alicia leaned out the open door. Mercs were already chasing the bus and there was a rear door too. Most were angling toward that. Alicia knew she should go and defend their weakness down there but she would never leave a team member behind.

If Russo failed to climb aboard she would jump clear and help him.

"C'mon Rob!" she shouted. "It's not hard to catch a bloody bus!"

Crouch eased up for a moment. Russo caught hold of the pole and heaved, Alicia tugging at his enormous arm as hard as she could. The behemoth was suddenly aboard and Alicia turned her attention to the men swarming up the narrow aisle from the back of the bus.

"Drive!" she shouted. "Don't let any more of these bastards get on board."

Crouch floored it, motoring up Piccadilly with The Ritz ironically now approaching on the right. Alicia met the first merc head on, catching a blow on the shoulder as she fought for his gun. A bullet went off, flashing overhead and exiting the front bulkhead. Kenzie clearly had no more qualms about gunfire in public areas, or at least her new underlings didn't.

Alicia broke the wrist and caught the gun, firing into her opponent's chest. Russo launched his entire bulk from the first row of seats, splashing down onto two more. Alicia fired at a fourth. Still more came

"Fucking servants of Kenzie," she complained. "Like friggin' cockroaches."

"You make them sound demonic." Healey fought to her left, engaging a merc on that row of seats. "Behold, the servants of Kenzie!"

"They are demonic," Alicia said simply as another merc launched himself up the bus's center aisle.

"We ain't servants," one of the mercs blustered. "We are our own men, freelancing to Bridget McKenzie."

"No, mate." Alicia said. "You're serving her in more ways than you can imagine and she's only gonna get worse."

Alicia smashed him to the ground, ducked as a gun was raised at the far end—one last merc alone. Healey and Russo fought to both sides. Crouch swung the bus intentionally hard down St James's street, cutting off a popular black saloon car with a grin.

"See how you like it."

Caitlyn blocked the way into Crouch's little cab, holding a pistol that had scooted across the floor and landed at her feet. Fateful perhaps, but lucky too. Her first shot blasted above a merc's head, coming nowhere near him but making him hesitate until Healey had a chance to engage. Caitlyn breathed a sigh of relief. The last thing she wanted to do was—

The merc struggled out of Healey's grasp, leaving him trapped between two seats and unable to give chase. Caitlyn saw the smirk stretched across the attacking man's face and knew instantly that he'd read her mind.

I can't shoot, can't even hurt someone in cold blood. Not like this.

As she vacillated the merc closed the gap. Up close he wasted no time swatting her aside as if she were no more than an annoying fly. Alicia saw it happen, saw the fear on Caitlyn's face, fear mixed with embarrassment. She fell away, crashing into the front seat and tumbling head over heels.

The merc had a clear run at Crouch.

Crouch knew it. As the man lunged he jerked the bus wildly, trying to throw him off balance. Suddenly the bus was swerving, tipping. Crouch had it up on two wheels as it swung around a corner. Everyone tumbled, shouting in surprise. Alicia thought she could smell burning rubber. Her vision tilted, the road ahead now slanted at an acute angle. The bus wrestled for traction, for stability. Still it tipped, almost at the point of no return, hurtling along and leaning over the oncoming cars. Alicia threw herself to the other side, hoping the weight might help, and saw Russo do the same. All she could do was hang on as physics played its part.

Crouch feathered the throttle, turning the wheel minutely to give the bus every chance to right itself. The merc pressed against his shoulder as if glued. A moment passed when all balance was equal and even the slightest gust of wind might have sealed their fate. Then the scales tipped and the bus began to come back down onto all four wheels, slowly as if savoring the moment. The merc squealed as he fell away and crashed in a heap against the door. Crouch saw a great chance.

Slapping at a button he hoped it would open the door whilst the bus was in motion. Luckily it did and the merc fell away into the night. Caitlyn clutched a pole to her chest as if she might never let go.

Alicia tumbled as the bus crashed down onto all four tires, but so did the merc she fought. Crashing to the floor he kept hold of his gun, now several seats in front of her and closer to Caitlyn.

"Don't be an amateur!" she cried at the young woman. "Help us!"

"I didn't do it on purpose!"

"Oh, that really helps."

Caitlyn now struggled to her feet, still waving the gun.

Alicia leapt up onto the back of the first seat and jumped from row to row, heading toward the back of the bus, her footing firm and sure. The merc scrambled. Behind her, Russo slammed his opponent against the side window, shattering the glass in the overlarge pane. Despite a groan of agony the man still fought against Russo. Crouch roared past a dawdling Micra, much to the surprise and disgust of its occupants, and turned hard left onto Pall Mall. Alicia missed her step and crashed to the floor.

"Oh, come on!"

The merc gasped too, striking his head against a pole. Russo finished his opponent off with an elbow. Healey took advantage when Crouch's driving caused his enemy to lose a pretty good chokehold and ended the fight, coughing hard.

Alicia rose and jumped over the final row of seats, at last face to face with her adversary. His gun lay on the floor at his own feet.

Alicia grinned. "Suddenly feeling inadequate are we?"

The merc struck. At that moment Crouch slammed on the brakes and swerved to the curb, veering across yet another car. Both the merc and Alicia fell in a heap, tangled together. The man was big and wore a heavy jacket that puffed him up even more. It also served to hamper his movements. Alicia struck hard at his ribs and liver, but the jacket protected him from every blow. Underneath, she twisted and jack-knifed her body, throwing him aside.

He came up with the gun aimed at her face.

Russo stepped in, slamming a boot at his neck and breaking bones. Alicia sighed and looked up at the big man.

"I had him."

Russo nodded and held out a hand. "I know. But you don't need to worry about it. Because you have friends."

Crouch's voice filled the bus. "We should get out of here now. Before the police decide to lock us up."

Alicia took Russo's hand and allowed herself to be lifted to her feet. "Cheers, Rob."

"Any time."

THIRTY TWO

By late the next morning the team had everything they needed. A night in an obscure, side-street hotel away from central London and close to King's Cross did nothing to heighten their enthusiasm, and Alicia came as close as she'd ever been to refusing to take a morning shower. In the end, with the lights off and the door closed to preserve dimness she managed it. When she set eyes upon Crouch the next morning she frowned.

"Couldn't sleep?"

"More important things to do," he said as they filed out of the cramped lobby and into a brisk, bright morning. "I decided we need a device."

Alicia raised an eyebrow. "Oh yeah? Dare I even ask?"

"Not your kind of device. My mind. The first task of the day is to decide which of the two arches we're going to concentrate our efforts on."

Crouch took a left up Euston Road opposite the great sprawling mass that was King's Cross Station and started walking. "We need a vibrometer."

Alicia thought about everything he had said. "What do you mean 'my kind of device'?"

Crouch waved it off. "A vibrometer is a laser radar vibration sensor that can be used to detect the presence of tunnels. Developed originally for the military some years ago it helped detect buried landmines and improvised explosives—IEDs. The sensor measures surface vibrations, analyses them, and then equates them to a library of target data to render a map of what is below ground. It can find anything from voids to hidden machinery."

"And you can pick one up in . . . where? Currys?" Russo asked.

"No. But there is an electronics shop down Tottenham Court Road that has international customers and handles some rather sensitive goods. Nothing strictly illegal, of course, just merchandise the stuffy politicians would rather you didn't have."

Alicia followed the boss past St Pancras and Euston Stations, turning left onto Tottenham Court Road. Healey voiced a concern over being famished and Crouch took a glance at his watch.

"Actually," he said, "we do have time for breakfast."

They chose croissants, poppy seed pastries and strong black coffee at Kamps before continuing on their way. Crouch entered the large electronics shop alone, leaving Alicia and the rest of the team to their own devices. Alicia watched the flow of human traffic, fascinated by the gym-goers, the dog-walkers, the workmen in their hi-vis jackets and the odd partygoer undertaking the walk of shame. When Crouch returned he held a plastic bag, straining at the handles. Without a word he indicated the closest underground station—Goodge Street.

Twenty minutes later they were exiting Marble Arch station and heading over to the arch once more. Crouch stopped before the high gates looking a little wary. "This thing isn't exactly small, but it is the latest tech capable of detecting voids hundreds of feet below the earth."

He pulled the device out of the bag. Alicia saw his problem. The machine was as wide as a dinner plate with two holes and cylindrical lugs and a narrow disc-ended snout. Crouch laid the snout gently against the ground and flipped a switch, looking intensely uncomfortable now as a swelling current of sound waves filled the air. Passersby looked over. Alicia found herself wishing she'd relieved one of the earlier workmen of his hi-vis jacket. At least then they might have looked the part.

"How long does this take?"

"Don't worry," Crouch's tone belied his words. "Eight to ten seconds."

"And the readout?"

Crouch straightened, holding the machine up. "Right here."

The screen displayed a series of multicolored sound waves. To Alicia they meant nothing. Even to Crouch they meant very little.

"Well, according to my crash course, this says that there are no tunnels running directly under Marble Arch. So the Central Line underground system that has a station back there," he waved down Oxford Street, "at Bond Street and then here at Marble Arch must kink away toward its next stop at Lancaster Gate. Boys and girls, there's nothing under here."

Deflated, they moved quickly away, retracing their steps of yesterday down Park Lane. "Let's take a taxi," Crouch said, holding his arm out. "In case London's CCTV surveillance system spotted what we were doing." He shrugged. "It's better than being stopped on the hoof."

Ten minutes later they entered the central island of Hyde Park Corner and walked toward the great Wellington Arch. Crouch waited as long as he could and finally, warily deployed the vibrometer. Then the group retired to one of the benches that dotted the area.

"What does it say?" Alicia craned over.

Crouch frowned at the readings. "Would you believe it? A tunnel does not run underneath here." He stared at the arch. "Three do."

Caitlyn bounced in her exuberance. "Three?"

"According to this they do. And if I'm reading it right, which admittedly," he shrugged, "is debatable." He pointed at the screen. "That one is the underground. It's huge. So the

Victoria Line runs almost underneath where we're sitting now with the road at our backs. But the other two?"

"I'm on it." Caitlyn checked her tablet hurriedly. "And here we go. Nowhere does it offer the information that Hyde Park Corner sits above anything but solid ground, but when you add the word 'tunnel' we get several items of information. It seems that a large tunnel was built under here in the 1950s to help channel the traffic fumes away. There's a vent over there," she pointed at the arch. "Actually inside." She shook her head. "These people and their secret subways."

Crouch read on. "The fire brigade still get on average three calls a year from the general public warning of a fire inside the Wellington Arch because of warm air and dust coming up through the massive hidden ventilation shaft," he said. "And yet they still keep it all quiet."

"You build one tunnel and say it's a ventilation shaft," Russo said. "You could easily build another. Or place it over an old one."

"No mention of a third," Caitlyn said.

Crouch followed the line of the mysterious third tunnel. "It heads directly in that direction to start." He pointed toward Hyde Park. "Which is interesting because isn't that building there Apsley House?"

"Wait," Caitlyn said. "I just came across this. An account of a man's visit to the Arc du Carrousel. He blogs 'it was exciting to take the underground passageways to and from the monument and feel as though you were a part of something larger'. So the Arc had tunnels too."

Alicia let them work, their brainstorming part of the process of discovery and idea generation. To know that even now they were sitting above a network of hidden tunnels was exhilarating. Hyde Park Corner sat over a secret tunnel and had done so for untold years.

What were these people hiding?

THIRTY THREE

"How many secrets of this nature does London hold close to its heart?" Crouch wondered quietly. "You have both Marble Arch and Wellington Arch constructed and designed as entrances to Buckingham Palace and then later moved. Is that a clue? You have the Duke's original statue placed atop the Wellington Arch, also later moved in favor of the quadriga. You have tunnels built alongside other tunnels and hidden by the simple fact that they're never spoken of. And by mis-information. What do all these monuments conceal? That old abandoned house up Piccadilly?" He pointed to where they could just see crumbling gates and a huge, decrepit, once-stupendous house left to rot. "Is it really empty or is that a clever façade? Thousands of brass nameplates on buildings up Mount Street and Aldford Street and all over Belgravia, companies that mean nothing to anyone and yet on the street outside sit Maybachs, Rolls Royces and matt-black specials. Secret clubs. How many tunnels are there? Underground stations not in use? Offshoots nobody knows about?"

Alicia was becoming acutely aware of the passage of time. She wondered if Kenzie and Riley might be out there, watching even now. "So what's the next move?"

"That arch," Crouch said. "We need to look inside."

Alicia tailed the group as they studied the inside of the Wellington Arch. Even to her it seemed larger inside than it appeared to be from the exterior. Crouch saw almost immediately that an undisclosed door could easily be secreted inside here, even with the inclusion of a police station. As they walked he pointed out the closed-off areas, giving them such a surreptitious wink that Alicia laughed.

"No Michael," she said. "That doesn't look creepy at all."

Exiting again into the warming day, Crouch spoke as he walked. "Question is," he said. "Where's the subterranean entrance and can we get to it?" He re-examined the readout from the vibrometer device.

Alicia scanned the area for hostiles. Russo hovered at her side.

"Wait. I never noticed that before."

Alicia turned. "What?"

"The direct line of our third tunnel enters Hyde Park, yes?"

Caitlyn jumped in. "Yes!"

"Well." He traced the line on a map of London. "Then it definitely goes directly underneath there . . ." He pointed at a remarkable old Bath-stone clad building with high spiked green-painted railings outside. "Apsley House."

Alicia shook her head, lost in the swamp of information. "And what's Apsley House?"

"The home of Arthur Wellesley, the first Duke of Wellington. The very man who beat Napoleon at Waterloo. Also knows as Number One, London. It stands right along our route."

"It stands alone," Caitlyn observed, again using her tablet. "The Duke's house. Surprisingly close to the place where his monument ended up, despite it being isolated on a traffic island and made hard to reach. It's where Wellesley entertained, strategized and lived for much of his life. It now contains his collection of paintings, porcelain, a magnificent silver centerpiece and . . ." Caitlyn gasped out a breath. "No."

Even Alicia looked around. "What?"

"A heroic marble nude of Napoleon himself! Standing three and a half meters high he holds a gilded Nike in his right hand and a staff in his left. It was originally displayed in the Louvre and then around 1815 transported here by the orders of the Duke after victory. The timeline is spot on for the dating of the Congress of Vienna."

"And it is still there?" Healey asked.

Caitlyn nodded. "One of the house's main draws."

"A Napoleon statue in the Duke's house?" Crouch said wonderingly. "Is that a clue to the Hercules being there too?"

"Oh dear, oh wow." Caitlyn squealed suddenly. "Remember the final part of the verse?" She reminded them all of the as yet unsolved riddle.

"By the Pillars of Hercules he endures, a part of the soil, hiding among New Arches envisioned, to the victor the spoils," Crouch recalled. "I guess we still need to find the Pillars of Hercules."

Alicia scanned the horizon as if expecting to see two great marble columns. Crouch set off in the direction of the spotless-looking old house, but Caitlyn's voice rooted them all to the spot.

"How about this? Apsley House, built around 1771 stands on the site of an old lodge that belonged to the crown. Immediately before the start of the house's construction it was occupied by a tavern called Hercules' Pillars."

The whole group stared in wonder across at Apsley House.

"That place was once a tavern called Hercules Pillars?" Crouch said.

"Yep. It was immortalized in print in the book *A History of Tom Jones, a Foundling* by Henry Fielding as the location where Squire Western resides when he first journeys up to London."

"Then the Napoleon statue might be more than the spoils of war," Crouch said. "Much, much more."

Caitlyn stared at him, still shellshocked. "You're thinking X marks the spot?"

Crouch grinned. "What could be better? A naked statue of

your nemesis and your country's vilest enemy, standing in your own home above the greatest treasure he ever owned, that you now possess? It's pure conquest. The perfect triumph."

"Even I have to admit," Alicia said. "There are simply too many coincidences for this not to be significant."

Crouch plonked himself down on the grass that bounded the Wellington Arch. "This does throw up several rather large flags though," he admitted. "If we're correct. Somebody knows what we know. Somebody of importance and in authority. And they're keeping the Hercules hidden for a reason, probably greed. Why don't they want it found? Is it still too precious for the masses? If so then I certainly don't agree with them."

Alicia watched him take out his cellphone and contact Rolland Sadler, their benefactor. Crouch explained the situation in terse terms and then listened closely to Sadler's decision.

"I agree. It should be outed. The solicitors can worry about the legalities and the precedents and wrongdoings later. And let's face facts—the bloody thing might even have moved on."

Alicia judged Sadler's reply to be of a doubtful nature. Crouch finished up with a promise. "We'll find it if it's there, Rolland. Be assured of that."

Then he scrutinized his team. "Looks like we're about to vandalize an English Heritage site. Any objections?"

They paid an entrance fee, Crouch grumbling about the cost and waving away a woman offering headsets. Alicia asked the way to the Adam Staircase.

"Just through the door there." A bespectacled woman pointed. "And don't forget to take the stairs to the first floor for the Waterloo Gallery. And the basement." She pointed ahead.

Crouch knit his brow. "There's a Waterloo Gallery too?"

"Yes. The Duke collected many paintings of his victories. Are you sure you wouldn't like a headset? Just one maybe?"

Caitlyn held back a sigh and offered her hand. When the headphones and machine were duly handed over and operations revealed the woman backed away. Alicia led the way to the Adam Staircase and then exclaimed: "Oh my!"

She stared at the enormous marble nude, fascinated. Napoleon appeared to be walking, with a robe of some sort thrown over his upraised left arm, the hand clasping a staff. In his right hand rested a victory standing on an orb, the pose making him appear to be offering the victory to someone.

Russo nudged her. "What do you think?"

"Me? I just wonder how often Napoleon really wore a fig leaf strapped to his bollocks."

Crouch shook his head despairingly. "Only you, Alicia. Only you."

"What?"

"In this house? Amongst these works of art and wonder and magnificent sculptures. As I said, only you."

"You get what you see." Alicia indicated herself rather than the statue.

"And don't we know it."

Russo grunted softly at her side, stifling laughter. Alicia realized she'd been duped. "Ahh, Robster. You'll pay for that."

Crouch quickly turned his attention to the surface on which the large statue rested. Flagstones, some cracked, surrounded it. No carpet. No wooden flooring. Caitlyn, listening to the recording, pointed out that the floor actually had to be strengthened to accommodate the weight of the statue. He checked the walls all around it, rapping his knuckles against the surface, but it was all continuous plaster. It was only when he walked around to the rear that his gaze settled on something.

"An air-con unit?" he wondered, pointing out a large, scruffy white box seemingly bolted to the wall.

Alicia came around to look but was immediately taken with Napoleon's perfect buttocks. "Now that's an ass," she said. "If only Kenzie were here. I'd tell her. Maybe even stuff her head between them."

Crouch winced. "I'd like to get a closer look at that—" He paused as a group of tourists came in and paused to admire the sculpture.

Alicia whispered. "Say the word. I'm sure I can say something that'll make them move along at a faster pace."

Crouch held up a hand. "Not necessary. I often find the art of lingering and mulling to be quite successful."

"Oh yeah." Alicia moved away. "Me too."

Crouch walked to the front of the room, taking in the entire picture. The tourist group moved on and then so did another. Several sniggering schoolboys on a school trip clattered by and, as they climbed the winding staircase, tried to reach out and touch the victory. Crouch returned at last, pointing now to Alicia's left.

"You see the blue unit there? It's what? A heating unit? A housing? See the black mesh."

Alicia stared toward the unit he indicated. It was large, affixed to the wall, with a flat top on which stood another carving and a plaque explaining the painting that hung above. "It's larger than the air-con box," she said. "Easily big enough to admit a person."

"Right. But let's not forget the basement."

Alicia stood bored as Crouch and Caitlyn dragged them downstairs and examined every inch, every painting and display case that resided at the bottom of Apsley House.

In the end it was easy for Crouch. "You spoke of coincidence." He rounded on Alicia quite suddenly. "You?"

"All right, calm down, Mikey. I'll take that one on the chin."

"No," he said, excitement making him tremble a little. "No. Look!"

He waved at the final display case placed in the furthest corner of the basement, between two walls, a square container running from floor to ceiling like a shaft.

"It's all in here. The display. Do you see? A print of Napoleon. The original victory from the hand of the statue upstairs. That one is a fake, so schoolboys can touch it without fear of damage. And here . . . Napoleon's death mask. And a print of St Helena, where he died. This is the display, the victory shelf. This is our X, the real triumphal shrine to everything Napoleon lost."

Caitlyn was on her knees, examining the pieces as closely as she could.

Alicia dropped beside her but concentrated on the floor instead. "Drag marks," she said. "Faint. It doesn't happen often but this cabinet comes away from the walls."

Crouch looked around. The room was otherwise empty, the basement and its several flights seemingly a step too far for most of the visitors. Of course, the majority of the house's riches were on the first floor.

"Do it," he said. "This is what we're here for. This is the end. We already have mercenaries and tyrants up our asses. Might as well have the local cops too. And if this leads to what I think it does . . . we'll be walking right on out of here with nothing to fear."

Alicia and Russo hooked their fingers over the cabinet's metal frame at the top and bottom. Together, they pulled, gently at first. When nothing happened and a camera-touting tourist wandered in, Healey caught his attention by stumbling over an uneven piece of flooring. The group waited a few minutes and then tried again.

"Steady," Crouch mouthed. "Steady."

Gradually, inch by inch, the cabinet moved. It had been

designed to be a problematic shift.

"Maybe this isn't the true entrance at all," Crouch said. "I can't see Mr. and Mrs. Dandy Upper-Class Rich Person taking the shaft, can you?"

Alicia grimaced, still pulling hard and wishing she had enough breath left to answer that one. The possibilities were endless, stunning, as attractive as a desert sunset. But then the cabinet pulled free and they were left looking at the perfect square of a black hole that disappeared into the earth underneath Apsley House and London. A waft of age and earth floated up, not entirely unpleasant.

Crouch practically capered to the front. "All right. Bloody hell, I'd give my right arm for a flickering torch."

Alicia had to grin at his geekish fervor. Russo puffed at her. "I s'pose we could use a rolled-up painting from upstairs," he dead-panned. "But that might land us in even more bubbling liquid."

Healey handed out powerful torches from his backpack, giving Crouch an actual lantern flashlight to help lead the way. Alicia descended second, the barrel of her torch held between her teeth and illuminating the rough walls in haphazard fashion. She estimated an easy descent of about ten feet before a tunnel opened out below. Crouch was already turning in place like a dog marking its territory.

"What's up?" She jumped down to find they were standing at a three-way tunnel junction.

"Just getting my bearings." He checked his Special Forces watch. "This is the tunnel we found earlier," he said. "Stretching into Hyde Park." He pointed. "And then that way to the Wellington Arch." He motioned. "Everything's in a straight line as per Paris and the Arc de Triomphe. Everything lines up."

"So what's in Hyde Park?" Alicia wondered.

"I don't know."

"And that way?" She stood at the entrance to the third

tunnel—one they hadn't found earlier.

"I don't know, Alicia. That way, the third . . ." He squinted. "Heads toward Piccadilly."

"It must run directly above the Victoria Line," she said. "That's why it didn't show up earlier. The vibrometer just picked up the bigger Tube tunnel. Now that's some clever concealment."

Crouch nodded slowly as the others climbed down to join them. "An important tunnel."

"Tube stops are Hyde Park Corner to Green Park to Piccadilly Circus," Caitlyn said. "What's up that way?"

"And which way's the treasure?" Russo rumbled. " 'Cause it ain't gonna take long before someone finds that wide open hole in the floor."

Crouch grinned. "To my mind there's only one possible place for the treasure to be," he breathed, almost overwhelmed. "That way. Right under the monument to one of our greatest ever commanders. Under the Wellington Arch."

The treasure hunters continued their unremitting search, bowed but not broken by adversity, marching between rough walls of cracked stone, beset by the rumblings of what could only be traffic both above and below, hemmed in by the earth and breathing air that might be filtered down from the arch above or even from the passage that led into Hyde Park, until they came to a passage that no longer looked coarse but instead looked grand and majestic, imposing and splendid. The walls moved away as their path widened out and dim lights appeared above. Something glittered in the darkness ahead.

Something glorious.

Something stunning.

And Michael Crouch fell to his knees in wonder as he approached.

Words were not enough.

THIRTY FOUR

The Hercules Tarentum was the greatest work of art of the greatest sculptor of the greatest leader who ever walked the earth. It was the only surviving work of that sculptor. It had been looked upon only by the privileged for untold centuries, and the cause of death and the shedding of rivers of blood, possibly the driving force for the entire sack of Constantinople. Consequently it was a spoil of war, plundered by conquerors and despaired at by the defeated. More than the Horses of St. Mark, it was unattainable.

But even these facts running through Michael Crouch's mind did not prepare him for the utter wonder of it all. It rose colossal, like a conquering Titan, climbing toward the vault of the ceiling and causing him to crane his neck up and up. Once in ancient times it stood on the acropolis of a Greek colony, as often visited by people as the famous spectacles of today. Spotlights glittered and shimmered all around it, set in stone and brick. Seated atop a bronzed chair, even his toes began at the top of Crouch's head. Glimmering golden shimmers gleamed from every facet, every plane of the body, limbs and head. Crouch felt his eyes dazzled by the shining lights and he couldn't move. Not even his mind worked properly.

Hercules sat upright and strong, a key in one hand and a cup in the other. His immense size, as well as stunning the senses, served to remind the onlooker of the man, the God himself, and of all the deeds he once accomplished.

"How on earth would they ever get something this size down here?" Russo asked.

Crouch found his voice for a second. "Just remember all the

construction, the tunnels built here and in Paris, and even back in Venice and Constantinople. The Hagia Sophia rebuilt again and again. St. Mark's Basilica rebuilt. Do you really think those and dozens more restorations were purely cosmetic? No, ostensibly they were to hide something else and new additions. And it is still done that way to this very day."

"So when you see St. Paul's or the Washington Monument or some important cathedral covered in scaffolding don't just think they're tinkering with the wallpaper?" Healey put forward.

"No. Think sinister. At least, that's what I do."

Alicia moved forward, even her bluster momentarily subdued by the fabulous treasure. The walls to his back had been covered by carvings and tiny sculptures. She now noticed a seating area off to the right. "Unbelievable," she muttered. "Your perception of this being a treasure of privilege was spot on. They even have their own little viewing area."

Russo craned his neck. "No Pepsi machine?"

"Sorry. It's probably Bring Your Own Bollinger."

Crouch finally roused himself. From his backpack he took a digital camera and proceeded to catalogue the entire area. Both Caitlyn and Healey did the same, preserving the pictures for later and providing backups.

"So what's next?" Caitlyn breathed. "Now that we've succeeded."

"It's time to bring this beauty to the world's attention." Crouch smiled at her. "We'll use the same protocols we used for the Aztec gold. Get Rolland involved. Find us someone in authority we can trust. But first we have to map out the rest of this tunnel complex."

Alicia backed away from the Hercules, feeling an urge to bow. The others followed slowly and they soon came back to the three-way junction.

"Let's try the one that heads toward Piccadilly." Crouch nodded. "That one intrigues me most."

Alicia led the way, following a new passage that began to descend at a sharp angle. Luckily the passage was wide and cobbled, affording excellent grip. Alicia also noticed filigree on the walls, lending the route an air of sophistication. Nobody spoke as the tunnel wound down and down, the minutes passing slowly. In the end, Alicia exited under a high archway and beheld what lay on the other side.

"Fuck me," she breathed. "I didn't expect that."

THIRTY FIVE

"Whoa." Russo pushed past her shoulder. "Is this . . . is this an underground station?"

Alicia nodded. "Yeah, and it sure as hell ain't on any Tube map."

Their path descended to a wide platform and a much wider tunnel that arrowed straight ahead, keeping up the direction they were traveling. The ceiling was a brick vault, the walls painted over yellowing plaster. No decorations were in evidence. The station appeared to be entirely functional and nothing beyond obligatory. The rails gleamed.

Crouch nodded at the train. "Are you getting on?"

Alicia studied the double carriage. To her, it appeared to be a standard Tube transport, complete with sliding doors and no doubt the tinny-voiced tannoy operator she could never quite hear. "I'm not really a Tube kinda girl."

Russo grunted. Crouch pushed past her and approached the train that sat as still as a mountain alongside the platform. As Alicia watched he reached out a hand to press the illuminated entry button.

The doors slid open instantly with a sound that reminded her of *Star Trek*. Clearly, the carriage was modern and well kept. She craned her neck around, trying to see further up the tunnel. Dim lights shone up there, revealing nothing but the cold stone-clad walls around them. All she could tell was, the track as far as she could see ran dead straight.

Crouch entered the second carriage, followed by Caitlyn and Healey. Alicia could see through the windows that the inside was similar to the standard arrangement except for the seats which were real leather and extremely plush. As she looked harder she saw bespoke champagne buckets built into the floors and seat pockets that held reading material. The floor was plush carpet. A red button beside every seat no doubt summoned a waitress. Alicia stepped onto the train.

Crouch moved into the first carriage and then approached the front. "A small driver's carriage," he called back, then popped his head through the door. "Shall we?"

Alicia liked his style. "Hell, yeah."

Taking the train to its terminus seemed the best idea. At the very least it would shed some light on to the prime mover behind this spectacle, this statement. The team grabbed poles in imitation of a normal Tube train before grinning at each other a little self-consciously.

"I don't exactly think it will be like the Northern Line at rush hour," Russo said.

"More like the Personal Shopper line at Selfridges," Caitlyn said.

Alicia spun as voices echoed down the tunnel. In another moment she saw feet and then Kevlar-jacketed bodies and hard faces. How the hell had Kenzie found them this time? She raised one of the guns she'd appropriated from the dead bus-riding mercs and took aim. Russo lined up beside her. Caitlyn screamed for Crouch to get the train started.

The engine juddered to life.

And the mercs piled on.

Alicia saw the glint of a flashing blade near the tail-end of the assault and knew that Kenzie had already found the Hercules—this then was her final onslaught.

All in, she thought, *for the win.*

An arm slammed down on her shoulder with crushing strength. Alicia took the pain and jabbed into the exposed armpit, drawing forth a shriek. Already another body was in her face, the vest of a tall man scraping her forehead. She brought a knee up, the close confines leaving her little choice, and felt him buckle. Realizing there was no way of stopping the mercs from boarding the still-unmoving train the Gold Team fell back to give themselves more room. A gunshot went off and a man fell between the train and the platform, hitting the tracks hard.

Alicia fired and ripped one of the champagne buckets away from its tenuous stand, using it like a baseball bat. Her target took the slam on the forehead. Blood spurted and flowed, spraying his colleagues as he collapsed to the floor. Others tripped over him. Alicia scrambled back to give them more room to fall.

At that moment the train rattled into motion. Its wheels gripped hard and a squeal emitted from the tracks below. Slow movement occurred. Those mercs left on the platform jumped for the doors. Alicia was torn—on the one hand wanting less enemies to fight but on the other unhappy about leaving them in the vicinity of the greatest treasure she had ever found.

Not that they could move the bloody thing.

But they could damage it. Losers often took to destroying or damaging that which they could not attain. The world suffered often and significantly because of it.

The train picked up speed. Mercs crowded down the second carriage. Alicia jumped onto a plush chair and fired, feeling a return bullet whizz past her ear. A window shattered. Another bullet thunked into the leather. She leapt over the end, gun whipping down and across the bridge of a nose. To her left Russo ran at them like a bowling ball, scattering them like pins. One man hit the window so hard he not only broke it, but fell through the resultant gap, dragged along between the rough wall and the train for a few meters.

Alicia winced. Even Kenzie, who she kept a constant eye on, flinched a little. Russo took advantage of his destructive rush and pounded on half-comatose men. In the end he had to launch himself headfirst to avoid a bullet.

The projectile pierced the roof of the train. Alicia noted Healey at her back, standing between her and Caitlyn. The ex-MI5 analyst in turn protected Crouch with a fully loaded pistol. Healey took a blow, but gave as good as he got. By now the train was rattling along at full speed and Crouch showed no signs of slowing down. Alicia estimated only half a dozen mercs remained back at the platform and, leaderless, they would probably fade away. Let them. The less people interested in the treasure the better for all of them.

Kenzie's blade ripped through leather at her side. Alicia was suddenly face to face with the relic smuggler.

"I always make good on my promises," Kenzie hissed.

"Really?" Alicia incapacitated another merc as she eyed her opponent. "Which gym did you choose?"

She sprang back as the blade sliced the air where her throat had been. Unbalanced by the bouncy, leather-bound seat she sprang back into the aisle. She moved forward. The train plowed on. The mercenaries advanced. Russo threw men left and right, took heavy blows and even a bullet to the side. Luckily, it only winged him, a scratch, nothing to write home about.

Then Healey cried out in pain. Alicia looked back. The young soldier was being forced up against a window by a merc with a meaty paw around his throat. Healey was off the ground, kicking wildly, disadvantaged by his position and unable to squeeze free. Alicia bounded over and smashed into the merc with a flying kick, sending him head over heels into the first carriage. Healey fell and choked. Caitlyn dispatched the merc with a pained grimace.

Alicia dragged Healey to his feet. "C'mon, Zacky boy. No one wants to die a virgin."

"I'm not a—"

Then Kenzie was upon them. A slice of her blade passed over Alicia's head and carved right through an upright pole, leaving the two ends sagging. A return chop missed Alicia's arm and thudded off the carpet, sending fibers into the air. Alicia smashed her boot into Kenzie's exposed midriff, sending her staggering into the seat and across the aisle.

In a second, Alicia was on her, straddling her lap, gripping the sword arm tight in one hand and punching hard with the other. Kenzie fought back the same way, trying to block Alicia's punches and jerk her other arm free. They traded punches as the train whisked them through the darkness.

Then Crouch began to slow. Alicia felt the deceleration and struck even faster with her free hand. The blows began to get through, bruising Kenzie's cheek, her forehead and then blacking an eye. Kenzie bucked wildly, trying to throw Alicia off but the Englishwoman only rode the waves.

"Yeehaw, bronco!" she cried, adrenalin pumping. "You're not much of a ride, Bridget!"

Kenzie rolled, finally realizing that to make any headway she would have to release her weapon. The blade thudded to the carpet. Kenzie swiped up with a free hand, catching Alicia by surprise. The constant bucking gave her some wriggle room. Then Russo collided with Alicia and the mercenary leader was free.

Alicia landed on the discarded sword, wincing, but luckily it was lying flat.

"Get the fuck off me, Russo!"

"My bloody pleasure."

Russo rolled just as the merc he was fighting punched downward. The blow struck Alicia on the bridge of the nose, making her see stars.

"Whoops." Russo tried not to smirk. "My apologies for that."

He heaved the merc away. Alicia rolled, seeing a new

attacker tackled by Healey before he could reach her. Standing up, she gripped an upright pole for balance. It took a moment for the stars to subside. By then, Crouch was slowing fast and the momentum of the train had ceased. All of a sudden the darkness that pressed down on the windows cleared and they shot into the light, emerging onto another platform. Alicia could see by the bricked-up tunnel ahead that they had reached the end of the line.

"Of course!" Crouch exclaimed loudly from the driver's carriage. Then he came crashing through the door. "What's in a direct line from the Wellington Arch straight up Piccadilly?"

"Michael, I'm a little busy right now." Alicia took a merc's head under her arm and squeezed him into submission.

"You know it!" Crouch shouted in his enthusiasm. "You saw it before. A playground for the privileged."

Alicia saw the doors that led to the platform sliding open. An archway stood off to the left and stairs beyond that. Double doors that might be an elevator. Benches coated in pure white leather, studded and decorated with bespoke carvings. A closed mini bar constructed in the finest dark woods.

An inconspicuous sign above the archway revealed all.

To The Ritz.

THIRTY SIX

Alicia jumped from the train before it had entirely stopped, dragging a merc along with her. She let him collapse to the floor and picked up his superfluous gun, then spun and took aim at the melee.

Another window shattered, but this time it was Russo lunging out of the way of Kenzie's sword. Both Crouch and Caitlyn advanced up the aisle, guns raised and firing when they saw a clean shot. A merc jumped out of the other carriage door and stared at her.

"Get down," she said with a warning in her voice.

Predictably, he came at her. She fired two shots into his vest and then rendered him unconscious. Kenzie attacked Russo on the train with the sword. Alicia saw it thrust through the shattered window. She ran to the door.

"Get your fat ass out here, Bridget! We have something to settle."

Enraged, Kenzie swung away from Russo and clambered toward Alicia. Backing away, she gave herself space out on the platform, probably a bad idea because it gave her opponent room to swing.

And maybe not.

Fighters who relied too much on a single move or a preferred weapon never understood that in addition to it being their great strength, it was also their Achilles heel.

Alicia allowed Kenzie a few practice swings, eyeing her all the while, both women circling. She threw her gun to the floor. She smiled into Kenzie's eyes.

"They're gonna love you in prison, Bridge."

Kenzie stepped and sliced the katana downward in shallow thrusts, again and again, each one aimed at Alicia's shoulders. There was no full swing, only stabs. Alicia danced aside, backing toward the archway and the stairs beyond in case she needed to reduce Kenzie's space. The tip of the blade sliced across the top of her chest, just tearing the jacket slightly. Kenzie changed the backswing into a sharp lunge.

Alicia didn't try to dodge, just judged and stepped back a little. The edge of the katana drove into her vest, penetrating hard but only so far. Alicia's perceptiveness was perfect. The blade stuck for a moment, throwing Kenzie off balance, its tip not quite reaching Alicia's bare skin.

Swatting the katana aside, she struck with devastating skill and speed. A heel into Kenzie's knee, the front of a boot to her sternum. Stepping in, she deployed missile-like strikes to more weak spots, making Kenzie's ears bleed as she slammed fists into them. A groan escaped the Israeli rebel. On her knees she tried to lunge for Alicia's discarded gun.

"Desperate to the end."

Alicia stood on the fingers, though careful not to break them. She was no sadist. Kenzie withdrew her arm quickly. Russo suddenly came lumbering up.

"You okay?"

"Oh, now you ask? When the crazy sword wielder's kneeling at my feet."

Russo skimmed the train with his eyes. "Just mopping up in there. So this is the end of the line, huh? The Ritz?"

"Who knows?" Alicia wondered where the staircase might lead. "Could be an old passage. The owners might not even know of its existence."

Crouch joined them. "Everyone okay, I see. Let's grab this piece of crap and head on up. And see what we can see."

Alicia reached down and, with Russo's help, took her time restraining Kenzie. At first, threat was simply not enough. The feisty Israeli gave as good as she got. Alicia saw a little of herself in the woman's eyes. *Shit, I need to bury that thought as far down as it will go!* Russo took a blow to the thigh; Alicia two to the head. In the end it was the gun that calmed Kenzie down, along with the mad glint in Alicia's eyes.

Calm the fuck down or I will shoot you.

The threat was clear between gazes. Clear as crystal.

Healey came up panting, Caitlyn alongside. The black-haired girl didn't realize she was spattered with blood and Alicia wasn't about to point it out to her. *Little steps,* she thought. *Taken one by one.*

Crouch passed through the archway, ignoring the elevator. Even now they might be on some kind of covert CCTV but the rising car would surely announce their arrival. The stairs were the better choice. He rose steadily, followed by his team. At the top the staircase opened onto a half-circle landing, constructed of stone and overlaid with Italian marble. The surface was slippery.

Before them stood a cage door like an old elevator, and beyond that a set of high double doors, clad again in Italian marble. Crouch paused. "This wasn't just built for the Hercules," he said. "I imagine the route between here and Hyde Park has existed for longer than we thought."

"Do you think the Duke utilized it this way?" Caitlyn asked.

Crouch pulled a face. "It's possible, but I'm doubtful," he said. "More like a secret group possibly even with connections to Napoleon and ancestors who viewed the Hercules back when Constantinople was of consequence. But I do believe he looked upon it. And that leads us to another point . . ." he glanced around at Kenzie. "How did you find it?"

"A door inside the Wellington Arch," she whispered. "Don't look so shocked. I know everything about you. Do you remember when your unit was destroyed?"

Crouch clenched his fists. "Of course. The Ninth Division

was ambushed, usurped."

"Save it. Because one man survived. One you left for dead."

Both Russo and Healy ducked forward now, having believed they were the only survivors. "Who?"

"I want a deal."

"Oh, for fuck's sake." Alicia pushed Kenzie toward the cage door. "You and your deals. Take a walk."

"One man knows all your contacts, all your moves. We knew what you knew almost as you knew it. Paris, London. The congress and the poem. You really need to learn to keep your mouth shut."

Crouch had almost stopped her, but now realized Kenzie would be better dealt with later. They waited for Russo to break through the lock and then pulled the cage doors apart. The high doors beyond had but a single lock near a single handle. Alicia pushed hard at the tiny gap.

The doors didn't budge.

"We may have a problem."

Crouch and Caitlyn cast around but found no way of opening the door.

Russo clicked his fingers. "One of the mercs was carrying a shotgun," he said. "I'll nip back and grab it."

"Cool," Alicia said. "And if it doesn't work we'll use Kenzie's ass to mow it into rubble."

Kenzie hissed at the Englishwoman. Russo moved off to a final call from Alicia: "Hope you don't get scared on your own, Robbie!" to which Crouch ordered Healey to follow in case any of the mercs had been faking.

Minutes passed. Alicia passed the time bating Kenzie and strapping the woman's sword to Caitlyn's back. At last Russo returned with the shotgun and angled it at the small lock.

"Take cover."

The boom resounded in their eardrums. The doors shattered apart. Alicia passed through the ruins very carefully, to find herself in an abandoned ballroom, emerging from behind the stage. They looked to the walls and saw no windows.

"Basement." Crouch nodded. "As expected." He studied the destroyed set of doors at their back. "Looks like it was concealed behind a hanging mural like the walls of the rest of the room."

How many other secret passageways lay concealed around them?

They trooped on, climbing more stairs and finally emerging at the end of a long corridor. The Ritz was extensive, one of the world's most prestigious and famous hotels. An icon for high society and extravagance it was well known during the war as a place where secret meetings were held.

Now, the team passed along a rich and sumptuously appointed carpet, following a winding corridor that appeared to be somewhere near the back of the establishment. A tour up a winding staircase and another two corridors and they began to hear the sound of hushed conversation and chinking of fine tableware. A waiter passed them by, at first confused but then quickly accepting, and then two more. Alicia whistled at the high chandeliers, the ornate trimmings and lavish flower arrangements.

Crouch stopped. "This is the Palm Court." He stood at the entrance to a luxurious restaurant. Cream-colored walls, gilded armchairs and gilt bronze mirrors greeted them. The clientele all spoke quietly, leaning over their tables or delicately prodding their veal sweetbreads and fruit soufflés. Alicia saw a path toward the exit.

"Shall we make a run for it?"

"I think so and quickly," Crouch responded. "All this excess is about to make me ill."

Kenzie leaned in close to Alicia's shoulder. "Wouldn't you

prefer to linger? Maybe grab some quail?"

It was so incongruous that it made Alicia hesitate. What the hell . . .

Then her gaze fell upon the table to their right. Somebody waved. Alicia made out the face of Daniel Riley.

Crouch stiffened.

Next to Riley sat Beauregard Alain.

THIRTY SEVEN

Riley rose and waved them over, greeting the team like old friends. Alicia realized they stood out like cocks at a hen party and not in a good way. Patrons of The Ritz were already eyeing them with distaste. Any other day she would make them wear their côte de boeuf but the presence of Beauregard had discombobulated her.

Crouch edged toward Riley, clearly expecting hostility. As they came closer Riley insisted that they take their seats. Beauregard sat in silence, staring down at the table.

Alicia made sure she sidled in beside him.

Riley showed them the napkin that rested on the table, and on top of the deadly Model M&P Smith & Wesson Bodyguard 380 handgun. Double action, it was a .380 auto and held six-plus-one rounds. Matt black in color, it lay like a predator waiting to pounce.

Riley grimaced at Crouch. "Thought you'd beat me didn't you? Well, maybe you did but I don't die so easily. And when Kenzie here told me where you were and all about this man—" he indicated Beauregard a little warily, hand hovering above the napkin. "We concocted a little backup plan."

The team were staring between Beauregard and Crouch. "You know him?" Caitlyn asked quietly. "What am I missing?"

Riley waved it away. "Doesn't matter now. You're probably going to be dead in a few minutes anyway." He pushed his half-eaten meal toward her. "Fancy some ravioli?"

Crouch banged the table hard enough to make the cutlery bounce. "What do you want?"

"Calm down, Michael. You'll get us all thrown out. Either

you or that bloody sword strapped to Caitlyn's back. Now, we all know how badly you wronged me. And we all know how badly I wish this tasty ravioli was your still-dripping liver. But this treasure? It calls to me, Michael. Like a mermaid riding a wave I'd just love to bone, it calls to me, singing in the sweetest of voices. The gold. It needs me."

Crouch cocked his head, struggling to follow. "Are you offering me Beauregard for the Hercules?"

"Oh well, if you want to put it that way." Riley stroked the topside of the napkin suggestively. "I want her too."

Kenzie actually looked a little unsure. "Yeah."

Alicia used their exchanges to send an inquisitive frown directly at Beau. In answer he raised cuffed hands, hidden beneath another napkin.

Riley caught Beau? I don't believe it. Nobody could catch Beau, not even the SPEAR team.

"You're wondering how I caught him aren't you?" Riley inclined his head. "Clever ole Beauregard Alain, the world's greatest assassin. Caught by Daniel Riley, the world's greatest—"

"Twat?" Alicia suggested quickly. "Bell end?"

"Careful, Myles. I could kill you all."

"Don't flatter yourself."

"Try me."

The world went silent. Riley stroked the napkin slowly. Alicia stared into his unblinking eyes. The truth was, he could certainly kill some of them. She could not save them all. The only modification here would be the passage of time. Something always came along to change the playing field.

She bobbed her chin. "How do you want to play this?"

"First, free me," Kenzie said.

"You're not tied, you dumb bitch. You're here because we have sights on you."

"I'm here because I want to be, *bitch.* You think a part of

216

this wasn't my plan?"

Healey stared at Crouch. "Doesn't Beau work for the Pythians?"

"I'll explain later," Crouch told him. "But he works for me. Always has."

Riley surveyed the restaurant, happy that all its patrons had returned to their meals. "Y'know," he said. "I love leading people on. Baiting them. Dangling the carrot and then using the stick." His face broke into a smile that could not reach his eyes.

"Kenzie," he said. "You brought all this to me. Gave me this chance. For that I thank you and hope taking the first bullet between the eyes is just reward."

The napkin lifted, the gun waiting. Kenzie's eyes filled with fear. Riley's hand moved fast. Alicia and Beauregard worked in silent partnership, heaving at the table from below and tipping it toward Riley. The gun slid backward and the man fell from his chair.

Screams rang out.

The restaurant exploded into chaos.

Alicia scrambled over the still tipping table top, balancing along its rim as carefully as she ever had in her life, and rose above the fallen Daniel Riley. Her problem was she'd located the Smith & Wesson and it was now aimed toward her.

Altering her flight she twisted away. The gun rang out, the bullet passing by. Alicia fell out of Riley's line of sight and then Crouch was crashing into him, knees taking him in the chest. Kenzie backhanded Caitlyn and kicked Healey between the legs, stunning them both. Russo raced to Crouch's aid.

Riley rose, grabbed a gilded Louis XVI armchair and smashed the oval back across Russo's oncoming bulk. The soldier covered up, going down. Crouch wrestled for the gun. It went off for a second time, the bullet entering the carpet and leaving only five remaining. Alicia pushed the handcuffed

Beau behind her and struck at Riley.

Outnumbered, the terrorist backed off, still trying to fling Crouch away. A thump to the ear helped. Crouch staggered, flailing at thin air. The gun aimed right at him and the shot went off.

Alicia hit at the very last moment, redirecting Riley's arm so that the bullet shattered a portion of fine trellis work. The gun spun off across the floor, skidding under a table. Riley stood alone for one moment.

Crouch squared up to him.

"Remember India!" Riley screamed. "Remember the worst of your fucking past, old man!"

Crouch visibly flinched. Alicia went suddenly immobile. Riley opened his jacket to reveal a string of small grenades, their pins all wired to a single pull switch. They were wrapped around his waist.

Crouch whispered. "You crazy son of a—"

"Crazy, yes! Imprisoned, no! They broke me, you fool. The SAS? They broke me and turned me into what you see now. That's why I left that day and never contacted you. That's why we stand here now. I couldn't go on, Michael."

"But you were already there."

"Not up here." Riley tapped at the side of his head. "Not where we truly live, Michael, and in my soul. They destroyed it."

"So why not just die like a good man?" Crouch played for time. "Or find a bloody normal job?"

Riley blinked at him, genuinely confused. "I did."

By now Alicia was behind him, with Healey and Caitlyn approaching slowly. Riley allowed them to come nearer.

"We go as one," he said. "The blast will be exhilarating, to know you are all there with me. Bonded at the end. Shattered together. Mixed together. Are you ready?"

Alicia thrust Beau away. There was no way she could stop

Riley from pulling those pins, only put her trust in the only one who held the slightest chance.

Caitlyn Nash.

The inexperience, the fear, the amateurishness she showed in the field. Their world depended on her now.

Riley smiled widely and looked up toward the ceiling's lion skin motifs as if seeking absolution. His finger tightened on the wire pull.

Caitlyn stepped closer.

Crouch fell away.

Healey caught their enemy's attention and Alicia said, "Hey!"

Caitlyn's window opened, both the shortest and longest window of her life. As Riley glanced away she drew the katana Alicia had strapped awkwardly to her back, and swung it all in one fluid movement. The blade whispered through the air, glimmering with reflected light, and chopped clean through Riley's arm, severing it above the wrist.

The hand struck the floor and bounced, because the katana had also severed the pull cord.

Blood sprayed and Riley screamed. With his other hand he tried to yank at the remainder of the cord but Healey had anticipated that and was close. Carefully, but firmly he held that hand tight, wincing as blood drenched his clothes.

Crouch stepped in and punched Riley on the temple; the man's body slumped into unconsciousness.

Alicia ran to Caitlyn and caught her in a bear hug. "Nice move, lady. Very nice move."

Caitlyn threw up down her back.

"Ah shit, I guess that's what you get when you're bringing up kids."

She kept hold of Caitlyn, knowing the woman would be experiencing all kinds of emotions right now. Fear. Hate. Self-loathing. Disgust. The list was endless and likely to alter her forever. After a while she felt a tap on the shoulder and looked up.

Russo's face blocked out all the light. "Kenzie's gone."

"She'll turn up again. We'll bag her later."

Crouch also came over and hugged Caitlyn. His thanks and gratitude went unsaid. "I thought we were all goners."

Caitlyn bobbed her head. "Me too."

"I'm thanking my lucky stars you remembered the sword."

"I didn't." Caitlyn shrugged in confusion. "Kenzie mimed it as she left the room."

Alicia backed away. "Probably best not to admit that. And now I need to change my top. Well, hell, The Ritz restaurant is as good a place as any."

She changed right there, beckoning a stunned waiter over and taking his jacket to cover herself. Sirens wailed outside in the street and flashing blue lights painted the apricot walls.

"Just what we need." Crouch smiled. "A bit of authority. Time to start the protocols, guys. The Hercules Tarentum will soon be available to everyone."

Alicia smiled as the cops walked in, their faces grim. "Calm down, boys. Do we have a tale for you!"

THIRTY EIGHT

Later, Alicia waited alone in her room.

The scene was set to her liking. Sitting in a small wicker chair with her back to the wall and the un-curtained window to her right she leaned forward, always ready to act. This particular hotel was almost the opposite of The Ritz; unimportant, unpretentious and almost unknown it perched among dozens more like it in an area classed as Camden. Her window looked onto a tatty roof and a rubbish-littered courtyard. A brick wall and a sooty chimney formed her best view.

When the knock came she was ready.

"Door's open."

Slowly, it eased inwards. A shadowy figure crossed the threshold and closed it gently behind him. Then he paused and stared in Alicia's direction. "Is there a problem?"

"How did Daniel Riley capture you?"

Beauregard to his credit stared down at the floor. "It is a sad, sad story."

Alicia lifted the barrel of her gun. "One I want to hear."

"You don't first want to . . ."

"No, Beau. I don't first want to. Maybe later, if I let you live."

The Frenchman came a little closer, his facial features now picked out by the dull light. Even that slight movement was full of sinuous grace and deceptive calm. Alicia gave him a warning nod.

"Come no closer. Do not underestimate me, Beauregard."

"Ah, it is so sad that we have to live our lives this way.

Either we fight or we quarrel or we fight or we hold weapons on each other. Is this the entirety of our relationship?"

"It's what we are. Now I want to know what happened today, who the hell you really are and who you're working for."

"It is a long story."

"I've ordered pizza."

Beauregard blinked. "Seriously?"

"Yeah. Money's on the table, tip included. When they knock just take it."

Beau eyed the bed. "May I—"

"No you may not. Now start talking."

Beauregard held up his hands. "Okay, okay. Riley conned me and it is not a proud moment. One I will not repeat. The man lured me here because he knew I was keeping tabs on Michael through a tracker, a final resort. When I entered the restaurant he showed me the grenades and threatened to detonate right then and there. I am sorry, Alicia. I really am, but I had confidence you and Michael would find a way."

Alicia carefully kept her surprise hidden. Beauregard never apologized for anything. This was a first. *Is he apologizing for making a clearly human decision or for letting me down?* An interesting quandary. "Go on."

"I am exactly who you think I am. An assassin, created by the French government long ago and then let go. What else could I do? Instead of fading away I honed my craft and came back deadlier. After dispatching those who wronged me I offered my services to the highest bidder. When that choice started to lead me down even darker paths I ran into Michael. It took some time but we agreed to work together. The rest as they say . . ." he spread his arms apart.

"And your agenda?"

Beauregard paused as the expected knock came and he paid for the pizza. When he turned back to the room Alicia was on her feet, gun leveled at his chest.

"What?"

"If you try even a slice I'll shoot you where you stand."

"Fine. My agenda, you say? Michael and I recognized the Pythian threat very early. Tyler Webb didn't just appear overnight you know, he's been soliciting people for years. When he finally pulled together his cabal we acted. I infiltrated their group and Crouch stayed close to your Drake."

"My Drake?"

"The Yorkshireman."

"Yes, I know who he is. Does he know about you?"

"Of course not."

"And now? Do you think your cover's blown?"

Beauregard chewed his bottom lip. "I don't know. Only Kenzie can expose me and it's difficult to predict what she will do. I think it is worth the risk."

"She could run straight to the Pythians."

Beauregard shrugged.

Alicia kept the pistol directed at his chest. "Hand me a slice. Oh, and take your clothes off."

She watched him, keeping hold of the weapon until he complied. Then she took a small bite of the cheese-covered dough bread. "You are right about what you said earlier. We are always fighting, sometimes literally, always arguing. What to do?"

Beauregard approached carefully. "Well if it leads to moments like this." He took her in his arms. "Perhaps it is not so bad."

Alicia pretended to struggle. "Now this is the kind of fight I like."

"And am I better than your newly discovered treasure?"

"Mmmm, I prefer my treasure naked, Beau."

THE END

Alicia Myles will return in Matt Drake 11—*The Ghost Ships of Arizona*—due for release early December 2015.

Her third and probably final solo adventure for a while will be released mid to late 2016 and will offer an ending for the Gold Team, of sorts.

Made in the USA
Columbia, SC
02 December 2021